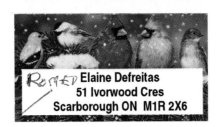

SHORT AND SWEET

Robert J. Fernandes

D1091457

HANSIB

Published by Hansib Publications 2008
London & Hertfordshire

Hansib Publications Limited
P.O. Box 226, Hertford, Hertfordshire, SG14 3WY, United Kingdom

Email: info@hansib-books.com
Website: www.hansib-books.com

A catalogue record of this book is
available from the British Library

ISBN 978-1-906190-19-4

Printed and bound in the UK

To my wife and children – you are not found in these pages because that would have been a long story.

ACKNOWLEDGEMENTS

I am grateful to Stanley Greaves for recognising the potential of my stories and encouraging me to write them down. Many thanks to David Ford, Edna Perry, Elfrieda Bissember, Philip Fernandes and my sons Dominic and Damian whose suggestions have been invaluable. Most of all thanks to the Guyanese people who have made my life worth writing about.

CONTENTS

Introduction 9

Mavis and Macaw 11

Mashramani Technology 15

The Card Receiver 21

The Raindrop 27

The Politician 30

The Short Story Writer 36

Angela 40

The Peer Tree 51

A Change of Heart 58

A Season for Stealing 63

The Old Tree 69

The Funeral 74

The Colour of Hearts 78

The Bogus Rastafarian 83

The Snail Hawk 89

The Strange Tribe 94

In God We Trust 99

An Immigration Affair 103

Donkey Experience 113

The Rainbow 119

A Set of Lights 122

The Old Dog 126

The Bird Watcher 130

Armed and Dangerous 137

The Old Hunter 145

Glossary 149

INTRODUCTION

"The Raindrop caterpillared himself closer to a particularly large group of drops in order to overhear what they were saying and without realizing it, he became an eavesdrop."

*I*n the hand of an accomplished writer the pen becomes a magic wand. It can create characters out of thin air, giving life to those that never existed before. Though I am fairly new to writing, I have tried to use some of this magic to unveil the unique social tapestry that is Guyana.

Short and Sweet is a collection of short stories and fables. Many of these stories have been taken from my actual life experiences, the fables on the other hand are simply a product of an overactive imagination and an ample supply of free time. The stories provide a brief glimpse of the traditional Guyanese way of life. From lost tribes to porknocker wives, from Leroy the laxative man to Ma Bancroft the gun toting old lady, they are all here sharing their new existence with Rainbows, Snail Hawks and Old Dogs. Some aspects of this life, like porknockers and donkey carts, are fast disappearing and need to be preserved as part of our cultural heritage.

Ever since I was a schoolboy I have been fascinated by the natural beauty of Guyana and as a young man it was my hobby to make trips to the more remote areas of the interior. On these trips I discovered a new Guyana, a Guyana that changed me forever. I returned from the interior with tales of savannahs extending as far as the eye could see, waterfalls that were higher than the lighthouse and funny stories about the people I encountered along the way. Since I already had the reputation of being a "Gaff-man", my friends were reluctant to believe the descriptions of my escapades. As a result, I began to take photographs in order to document my amazing discoveries. However, the tales themselves remained in oral form and became a tradition at family gatherings and parties, both at home and abroad.

In 1994, after repeated requests from friends over the years, my first story entitled 'The Old Hunter' was transferred to paper. The others were written intermittently over the next fourteen years and it is perhaps fitting that my most recent story entitled 'Armed and Dangerous' was written in the turbulent times of 2008. However, many of these stories became popular with my friends long before they were ever written down. As early as 1973, 'Donkey Experience' was a nostalgic favourite of Guyanese living in Toronto, although it was never written until 1995.

During the writing of these stories I became well acquainted with the main characters, some of whom remain close friends to this day. In fact, I judge the success of my stories by the level of concern I have for the characters after the story is over. I often think about their lives, and how they have changed mine. For instance, thanks to 'The Raindrop' I now try to avoid large groups for fear of eavesdropping. With this book I hope to introduce these characters to the world. I have really enjoyed meeting them all, and I hope that you do as well.

Robert J. Fernandes, 2008
Georgetown

Mavis and Macaw

*T*he small aircraft came to a stop in a cloud of dust at the end of the interior airstrip. It looked like some strange insect from the surrounding forest and seemed awkward and out of place on the ground. I was standing under an open-sided shed along with a group of porknockers. These men were partners, as their friendship had been forged in the crucible of danger and hard times, over many years. Laughing and joking with each other, they were in good spirits, eagerly anticipating their long awaited trip to their gold claim near Potaro river head.

The plane door opened and a short, large woman dressed in an old Guyana Defence Force uniform, was having trouble breaking free of the doorway. The door of this small plane was only designed for loading and unloading bags of sugar, rice and forty-five gallon drums of fuel, so it couldn't really handle Mavis. She appeared to be an enormous G.D.F. duffle bag with a head on it. She eventually sat on the floor of the plane and by passing the steps made, what was for her, a giant leap to the ground.

As the dust cleared, one of the porknockers called Rasta, recognised her and said to the leader of the group, "Macaw, dat is not you sweet-oman Mavis? What she doing here?"

Macaw was a tall, lean man with a small head and I guessed that he got his name from the way he walked. He was badly parrot-toed and leaned forward when he walked, as if he didn't want his tail to touch the ground. He should have been as surprised to see Mavis as they were, but he wasn't. This caused the other porknockers to realise that something was up and they all turned towards Macaw for an explanation.

Yankee-Tom was the first to speak. "I hope yuh know she en going in no backdam wid we?"

"Who gun liff she up dem bumps in de trail?" asked another one of the group, called Granpa.

Coolie Ally mumbled to himself, "I shudda bring me chile mudda."

Rasta said nothing and was still in shock as he stared disbelievingly at Mavis who was getting larger as she came towards them.

She waddled into the middle of the group, and as she turned to kiss her man Macaw, some part of her touched each one of them. The hairs on Macaw's neck seemed to raise slightly, either because he was glad to see Mavis or in his anticipation of the battle with his partners that was about to begin. In his most commanding tones he declared, "Somebody got fuh do de cooking wuk. Las time Granpa do um, he cook pure stupitness. Anyway Mavis gun cook and she gun get de same share as all awe."

All hell broke loose. As I drifted away from the group, I could hear the shrill voice of Mavis, like a baboon's call, high above the tangled voices of the others.

Sunday morning I was sitting on the bank of the Ireng River where I lived, trying to catch some fish. However the fish were all probably attending whatever holy services fish attend on Sundays and the only things biting were the atheistic Kaboura flies. As I watched the floating leaves go by on their journey to nowhere, the river seemed upset that the wind had disturbed the reflections on its surface so early in the morning.

In the distance the unmistakable, rhythmic tap-dance of paddles on the side of a corial, became slowly louder as three corials rounded the bend in the river and came towards me. It was Macaw and his crew of porknockers from the airstrip yesterday. Two of the corials were loaded with men and supplies and the other one was overloaded with Mavis alone draped across its middle.

Sebastian, an Amerindian friend of mine was paddling Mavis's corial and I could see that he was under pressure. Amerindians have an instinctive rhythm when paddling. To them it is usually an effortless exercise that can be kept up all day. Mavis however, had Sebastian completely out of tune. It was not so much her weight, though it would have helped to have cut her into quarters like the tapir he had shot last week, and distributed her more evenly in the boat. The real problem with Mavis was that she had absolutely no sense of balance whatsoever and Sebastian had to use all his skill just to keep the corial from overturning.

As one of the boats passed near the bank where I sat, I called out, "Yankee-Tom, you all running late. Sun high already and you ain't even reach first falls yet. What happen?"

"Wa happun," growled Yankee-Tom, cutting his eye on the boat with Mavis which was now lagging behind, "It still happunin." He then gave the loudest "suck teeth" that I have ever heard. It not only echoed across the river, but he dislodged his "false teeth" in the process and he had to struggle to keep them from falling overboard. As the corials slowly disappeared from view, I knew that the "Mavis Affair" was far from over and I had an urge to accompany the porknockers to the backdam so as not to miss the ending of the saga that would surely play out there.

Late one afternoon about two weeks later, my wait was over. I was tending my kitchen garden and listening to the gentle clicking of the Ite Palm leaves as they reported on the state of the wind in the Cipo valley, when the dark speck of a man floated down the grass-covered mountainside, and came slowly towards me. It was Rasta, or more accurately, what was left of him. Although I was accustomed to seeing porknockers after they had been walking for weeks on the trail, even so Rasta was in bad shape and looked somehow strange.

His fancy Brazilian jersey resembled a spider web designed to catch insects, which seemed to have caught a large animal instead. His black serge pants, once worn to church on the coastland, was not cut short in the usual way, but just seemed to have melted away above the knee. Instead of a belt around his waist he had tied a strip of frayed hammock, to keep his pants up. But it was the wild expression on his face that intrigued me most. "What happen to you Rasta?" I asked in eager anticipation.

Like a mountain stream after a heavy downpour, the drama burst from the angry, broken man. "Is not wa happun to me, is wa happun to all awe. Is dat balopshous Mavis, she like Manatee, she clumsy pun lan. Wa she en bruk she bun."

I sneaked a closer look at his clothes and noticed for the first time definite evidence of singeing.

"We camp was bout fifteen minit from where we does wuk, and one day we leff Mavis fuh cook we food and we gone fuh wuk. Nex ting we see is Mavis come running and tumble down pun she face inside de pit where we diggin. Over five minit she cant talk and all awe stan up round she waitin. I tought she was gun dead," Rasta stamped his feet to chase the flies, and it was only then that I noticed that he had no shoes and most of his toes were worn and bleeding.

"At lass she tell we dat de camp ketch-a-fiya an she cant out um. Accouri couldn't a ketch we. I feel like me foot en touch de ground till me see de fiya. It tek over de hole camp, but I fly strait fuh me hammock and warishi. De warishi dun bun up and fiya pun de hammock, but I scramble um and run back outside."

As he related the experience he became so worked up that he was panting. "De fiya from me hammock ketch me clothes and nearly bun me up. Ah loss everything."

I enquired about what had happened to the others.

"Dem scatta like wile hog in de bush, me en know where dey deh. Me en mine me tings bun up so much, but wa make me wan kill Mavis, is when me locks bun off."

Suddenly I realised why it was that Rasta now looked so strange. His rasta dread-locks that had taken him years to grow and had been his pride and joy for so long, had been completely burnt off. On closer inspection his hair now resembled a clump of razor- grass after a savannah fire. It was just ashes clinging to roots. I looked into the eyes of the hairless Rasta and finally understood the wish to murder Mavis that I saw burning brightly there.

Mashramani Technology

*L*eroy Chance was a person whose rough appearance could in no way mask an intelligence that was instinctive. As a result of his inquisitive nature, he had managed to overcome severe difficulties and absorb a good secondary education. He had tried various jobs at the places where school leavers with his qualifications usually found work, but the discipline of working at banks and insurance companies was not his style. The regimentation of office work was not only distasteful, but also failed to provide an outlet for his creativity.

Eventually, Leroy decided that his success lay in buying and selling, so he sub-let part of a stall belonging to a friend outside Bourda Market. After a few weeks of struggling to make ends meet, however, he realised that a stall holder was simply another name for a desk worker outdoors, as he had to sit and wait for customers to come and buy. He gave up his place in the stall, made a large tray and became a travelling salesman, or as he liked to refer to himself, an "agent of continuous commerce". He would now be able to go wherever he wanted instead of waiting for customers to come to him.

He had learnt in school that whatever profession you chose in life, if you really wanted to be successful, you had to specialise at it. Leroy made up his mind that his tray would have only one type of merchandise, but his problem was choosing the field in which to specialise. Before he could make his decision fate took a firm hand in Leroy's future. A neighbour of his, who was also a seller in the market, became seriously ill and gave Leroy his goods to sell for him. To his surprise the merchandise consisted entirely of laxatives.

It was a timid Leroy who put the leather strap around his neck that first morning and ventured into the market place with his tray full of senna pods, cascara, caster oil and a wide assortment of salts. Embarrassed at first, he avoided all female customers, but since they were in a majority, it was bad for sales. However, he quickly overcame his shyness and after a few housewives stopped him to make their purchases, Leroy the Laxative Man was successfully launched into business.

He quickly noticed that many of his customers did not only need laxatives, but also inquired about medicines for diarrhoea. While the laxatives he sold had a more local flavour, Leroy decided he would stock the latest diarrhoea medicines that he saw advertised on television, like Imodium AD and Mylanta PM. He was sure they were all excellent drugs because they all had letters behind their names and he mistook this to mean that they had received some national award in their countries of origin. With this new and complete range of merchandise, Leroy now boasted to everyone that he had now become a "Bowel Behaviour Specialist".

Everywhere he went he became very popular as people enjoyed his humorous calls designed to boost sales.

"Come on ladies let me organise your movements. Free up yourself and feel good," he would say as he approached a group of shopping housewives. If he saw a mother walking with children in the market, he would tell her, "Mummy I think you need me. Its green guava season again and you know how that does cause problems with little children bowels."

He also had multi-purpose calls like, "Whether you moving or not, let Leroy handle all your bowel arrangements."

When Leroy read in the newspapers that the Internet had at last come to Guyana, he was determined to gain access to it. He realised that this was an opportunity for him to learn about life in other countries of the world without having to deal with the problems of "Backtracking". While in school he used to spend many hours pouring over old, dog-eared encyclopaedias in the school library, trying to squeeze every drop of outdated information out of them. Since leaving school he had missed having his teachers to fill in the gaps in his knowledge by answering the multitude of questions he had about life in general. At last, with the help of the Internet, he would have access to the latest developments worldwide, in whatever field he chose. He would be on the cutting edge of Communication Technology. Although computers were very expensive, Leroy made up his mind that somehow he would raise enough money to buy one and get online.

In an effort to save money for this project Leroy became quite miserly. He even stopped buying drinks and "Fat Fowling" the girls at the Corner Kick Beer Garden where he hung out in the evenings. No matter how he tried, the money that he saved was nowhere near what he needed for a computer. Instead of getting nearer, the Internet seemed truly beyond his financial grasp. The annual Mashramani celebrations were about to take place and Leroy heard that the lots on the Mall, along the parade route, were being rented out as usual. He felt that this might be his only chance of raising funds for his project, so he rented a spot near the roadway where the bands would pass.

Leroy realised that it would make no sense for him to sell the usual beers and cook-up that other stalls would be selling. He would have to come up with something new. This problem bothered him for some time until one day, while passing an electronics store in Robb Street, he saw the answer staring back at him out of the display window. In an effort to advertise their television sets, the owners of the store had mounted a video camera to record the passers-by on the pavement. All those standing in front of the window could see themselves on the TV set placed there for that purpose. Leroy knew that Guyanese people liked nothing better than to see themselves on TV, and immediately decided that his stall on the mall would have to go high-tech. Besides selling the usual refreshments he was sure that the Mash trampers, after seeing themselves dancing and wining on TV, would want to buy a videotape of their performances.

Like all master plans this one had major mobilisation problems. Leroy did not have a TV set, video camera or video recorder. He, therefore, had to find someone who would be willing to lend him this equipment. The only person whom he knew well, that had this type of equipment, was his Uncle Aubrey who had just re-migrated from New York. His uncle prided himself in being the only high-tech member of Leroy's family and was always encouraging him to get into this field. He had told Leroy that he should stop "skylarking" in Bourda Market and become involved with the latest electronic technology, as that was where the real money was.

Uncle Aubrey was no match for the slick presentation of Leroy's proposal. He told his uncle that he was finished with Bourda Market and had decided to take his advice and get into electronics. Leroy outlined his Mashramani venture and assured him that it was only a pilot project, that there would be even greater things in his technological future. All he needed was the loan of the equipment and not money, as his uncle had feared. Uncle Aubrey smiled as he realised that he was trapped by his own advice and, against his better judgment, handed over his expensive video equipment to his enterprising nephew.

On the day before Mashramani, Leroy set up his stall at the corner of Church and Irving Streets and proudly painted a large sign on the front of it, which declared, "Mashramani Technology Centre". The other stallholders who were setting up their own stalls, all wanted to know what this meant. Leroy kept his secret, afraid that someone might copy his idea.

Mash Day came properly dressed for the celebrations in bright sunshine and blue skies and Leroy felt it would be a good day for video-graphing. As the first steel band drifted slowly up Church Street, even the stately royal palms lining the parapet forgot their breeding. Like giant green spiders on grey pedestals, they danced to the calypso rhythms of the breeze. The first two bands passed Leroy's stall without paying any interest. In the third one however, one of the revellers knew Leroy from the market and asked him what he had for sale. A group of trampers from this band then converged on the stall, and immediately seeing themselves on TV, increased the pace and antics of their dancing. Before they left Leroy had sold them five videotapes. He realised that the hardest part of the operation would be to keep the customers moving once they had finished making their tapes. This was the only way business could run smoothly, making way for the seemingly endless stream of customers prancing along the road.

All Leroy's friends from Bourda Market eventually discovered his location, but instead of boosting sales, it had the opposite effect. They all congregated in front of the TV and refused to move. A few of them asked Leroy for a special "market people" price, but the majority felt that they were entitled to freeness. The confusion they caused was preventing genuine customers from patronising the Mashramani Technology Centre and eventually Leroy had to give them two free tapes to get rid of them.

Many of the tapes Leroy sold were destined for relatives living abroad and therefore every effort was made by the local trampers to be as impressive as possible. Leroy had anticipated this and, for a small fee, provided an added service of props to enhance their images. He would furnish empty Budweiser beer cans to replace the bottles of local beer that the dancers held while the videos were being shot. Some times he even lent customers the empty Video Camera case to sling over their shoulders. Tee-shirts with the official Mashramani logo could be rented, if the revellers were not dressed in costumes. Leroy also had a powerful tape-deck with all the latest calypso hits to provide them with a wide selection of background music for their videotapes.

By late afternoon Leroy estimated that he had made enough money to finance his project and he was tempted to close down his operation. However the celebrations were in full swing and there was no shortage of customers. By this time the groups of people that came to the stall varied only in their degrees of intoxication and what should have been quick business, took much longer than necessary. Arguments and disorderly behaviour were the general rule and Leroy had to use all the people skills he had developed around the market, just to avoid fights breaking out.

A particularly large, disorderly group, dressed as Roman gladiators and in the advanced stages of drunkenness, arrived at the Technology Centre. Their leader was a tall, muscular man called "Teargas". Leroy knew him to be a very loud and troublesome man when he was sober, but with a day's share of rum and calypso music in his brain, he was almost unmanageable. He was so drunk that he had trouble standing still and swayed continuously to some alcoholic rhythm that only he could hear. "Teargas" organised his group to dance in front of the camera and then sat down in front of the TV, "flatty" of High Wine in hand, to watch the show. This would be Leroy's biggest transaction of the day as "Teargas" had ordered tapes for each member of the group. Leroy would definitely close shop after they left.

Between sips "Teargas" kept his eyes fixed on the TV screen as if he were looking for something in particular. As the gyrations of the group reached a climax, he at last found what he was looking for so intently. The speed with which "Teargas" rose from the ground made Leroy realise that he was not as drunk as he had made himself out to be. With a great roar of vulgar expletives he lunged into his group of friends and caught hold of the man he had seen hugging up his wife on the TV screen. Pandemonium broke loose. Women scattered screaming as the two men grappled in drunken rage.

Dressed for the part in their gladiator costumes, they seemed locked in mortal combat. The TV set was the first to go, side swiped by the tumbling men, it was knocked off of its stand and crashed to the ground with its screen smashed.

Up to this point in the proceedings Leroy had stood frozen in fear and disbelief, but the destruction of the TV Set galvanised him into action. He jumped on top of the two men in an effort to part them and prevent any further damage. This action was interpreted by the other drunk men in the group as a signal to start a free for all. They all piled on top of the three struggling men in a tangled mass of drunken, flailing humanity.

By this time Leroy found himself close to the bottom of the pile and was savagely bitten on his left ear. Just as he squeezed himself through a small opening between the mass of sweating bodies, he witnessed the total demise of the Mashramani Technology Centre. The brawlers had broken the main upright supporting the shed and this heavy structure came crashing down on top of them. It succeeded in extinguishing the conflict and the bruised combatants slowly untangled themselves from each other and the collapsed structure.

With tears in his eyes Leroy picked through the rubble like a fire victim searching for anything that could salvage his future. Eventually his worst fears were confirmed when he came across the remnants of his Uncle Aubrey's battered equipment. There was nothing electronic about it now as the video recorder had been impaled by one of the rafters and the camera had been completely flattened by the shear weight of the shed crashing on top of it.

Leroy was in a trance as he retrieved the cash he had collected during the day. He found a quiet place and sat down to count his takings. By his calculations, if he managed to get generous discounts, he might just have enough to replace the equipment he had borrowed from his uncle.

Thoughts of the Internet seemed so far away that he could barely bring himself to think of them any more. However, there was one fact of which he was sure, Mashramani was not yet ready for the introduction of technology.

The Card Receiver

*L*ouisa Row itself gave the impression that it was quite proud that it led to the Le Repentir burial ground. In fact it seemed annoyed at being interrupted by lesser streets such as Bent Street that were going nowhere in particular. Mrs Walcott had lived here for 'umpteen years', in a small, almost transparent cottage. She often referred to it as a wood-ants barracks. It was the kind of house that, in case of flooding, had warped pieces of board laid out in the yard, leading the way to both front and back steps. She was popular with most of the residents of Wortmanville, to whom she was known simply as Old Lady Wally.

When she was much younger Old Lady Wally was married and had produced two children in quick succession. When they were born she had told her husband, "The girl is yours and the boy is mine, now don't bodder me 'bout making any more children." Sadly her husband had died soon after, leaving her nothing but the two small children to be raised.

Old Lady Wally was already accustomed to sewing her own clothes, but was then forced to become a full time seamstress. Most nights she worked into the early hours of the morning, sewing dresses for sale to department stores or private clients. As the sole provider for her family, she had thrown herself into her dressmaking with a vengeance. She had to be independent somehow, not only as a matter of pride, but to show her well-to-do relatives who had disowned her for marrying a poor man.

The Old Lady had eventually come to love dressmaking. Although it kept her very busy and she couldn't get around much, all the latest gossip came to her through the kind courtesy of her customers. It was very amusing that sometimes the very rumours that she herself had started, would come back to her after making the rounds, so "hemmed and gathered", that she had trouble recognising them. But dressmaking

21

Old Lady Wally's house

also had its stressful side. Everyone wanted their clothes done immediately, especially at the Christmas season.

The miserly women, who only bought cloth when it was on sale, really annoyed her. They would expect her to make shimmering evening gowns out of the cheap "counter cloth" which had been in the store too long and massaged by hundreds of hands. Worst of all were the really fat women, shaped like box kites. They always chose the most sleek, hip-hugging styles from her fashion books and expected Old Lady Wally to make them fit. When she was not in a good mood, she would suggest that they go to church on Sundays and pray for a change of shape. After all, she reasoned, it was God that had made their shapes in the first place, and she was only trying to disguise them.

The Old Lady's two children grew up and started to work. Although this was a big help to her, times were still hard in the country as a whole and like many other young people, her children dreamed of migrating to North America for a better life. The Old Lady refused to even consider an existence without them, until one day her son came home and excitedly told his mother that he had managed to get an American visitor's visa and would be leaving shortly for California. He planned to stay there illegally and quelled the Old Lady's protests by promising to send for both her and his sister as soon as he got organised. A year later he sent an airline ticket for his sister, and she in turn promised to send for her mother as soon as she became organised.

After a few years of waiting, Old Lady Wally had come to the conclusion that America was not a very organised place. She was now like a ship without a rudder. The two stars by which she had steered her life were gone and she drifted aimlessly from day to day without a reason for living. As she got older she could barely do enough dressmaking to support herself. The children had promised to send US money for her, but maybe they hadn't gotten organised as yet. Old age was just like a dress she thought; as you grew older life seemed to fit you tighter. In her case, things were as tight as they could possibly get.

What Old Lady Wally needed most from her children was to be a part of their new life in America. After all, ever since her husband had died, their three lives had become fused by the relentless struggle for self-preservation. Like so many other parents who had been torn from their families by the plague of migration that gripped the country, she felt undeservedly cheated.

The Old Lady lived for the days when she would receive letters from her children, but these became less and less frequent. Instead of letters she received Birthday cards, Christmas cards, Mother's Day cards, Valentine's cards, Halloween cards and, occasionally, Get Well cards. All the cards were signed in the same touching way, "To the Greatest Mother in the World from your loving children." She had become a "Card Receiver".

Like any devoted mother, she always worried about her children and wondered if they were taking proper care of themselves. She wondered if their neighbourhood was safe from all the violence that seemed to be an every day occurrence in America. They could never imagine how necessary this information was for the preservation of her sanity. When a mother cares children so well for so long, it becomes her right to know everything about their lives.

Whenever she received a card from her children, the Old Lady would open it, shake it out and, with a smile that temporarily smoothed the wrinkles of her brow, would say, "Those dogs at the Post Office thief the US that my children send me again. I hope the next card they send is a credit card." When she hadn't heard from them for a long time, she would try to disguise her hurt with cynical remarks about them to her friends. "Instead of making them two children I shoulda make two dice and throw them, I mighta win something. Or better yet if I had make two sheep, you know how much sheep I woulda got by now?"

Old Lady Wally now spent so many hours with her eyes glued to the Jalousie louvre windows at the front of the house that the neighbours used to say that her face was sunburnt in stripes. From this observation post she liked to watch the parade of life and death that passed along Louisa Row every day on its way to the burial ground. From her discreet vantage point, very few happenings in the neighbourhood escaped her notice and she gave a running commentary on whoever she saw. "Wait she get baby already? It sure is not she husband own. All the same mixed people could get away with anything, whatever mischief they do their children could only come out mix."

However, it was funerals that especially interested the Old Lady. Having paid special attention to the Death Announcements on the radio the night before, she liked to play a game of trying to guess who the occupant of the hearse was as the funeral passed her house.

One day she recognised the funeral of someone she knew and commented, "Look who passing all dress up and only two cars following the hearse. Imagine, he used to play big shot on me. I sure if I was to dead now I would get more than two cars."

One Christmas, Old Lady Wally got a large package from her daughter. She opened it with great excitement, but it was only another large Christmas card. It was the kind that smelt of perfume and played a wordless melody when it was opened. On Christmas Eve day the Old Lady was summoned to a neighbour's house to receive a telephone call from her daughter. She answered the phone eagerly, only to hear her daughter in tears declaring how much she loved and missed her mother. Eventually her daughter asked her how she was making out for the season. "Well," the Old Lady answered, "is a good thing you send that big card the other day, because I going make soup with it for Christmas." Her daughter became hysterical over the phone and it took her mother quite a while to calm her down and get a chance to speak. "Look, I think you should stop crying, put down the phone and send the money that you wasting on this call. I love you too darling," the phone call ended.

Not long after this incident Old Lady Wally received a letter from her daughter. She felt the thickness of the envelope and thought it might contain photographs of her children. The old lady tore it open excitedly and to her surprise several small pieces of crushed, yellow stationery fluttered out on to the table. The envelope also contained a short note written on white paper which said, "Dear Mom, sorry about this, but when I had finished your letter, my pet dog Gemini, got hold of it and chewed it up. He is a naughty dog sometimes. Luckily I managed to collect all the pieces, so you shouldn't have any trouble putting them together again, your loving daughter."

The Old Lady could not believe her eyes. She stared at the frayed pieces of paper that lay on the table mocking her, and somewhere deep inside her fragile spirit crumbled. Her tears blotched the handwriting making it even more difficult to reconstruct the mosaic of her daughter's disrespect.

The letter finally gave up its coded message. Her airline ticket was on its way. This should have been a day of rejoicing for the Old Lady, but for the first time she questioned if this family reunion in America was really a good idea. She had lost her enthusiasm for the trip to the place where pet dogs seemed to have more rights than aging mothers. She reluctantly began to sell her household possessions. She remembered a friend of hers who had sold all her furniture while waiting for the ticket from her children, and was left sitting on a drinks-box in the middle of her house. She didn't want this to happen to her so she would have to be careful.

At last the ticket came and the only things she had left to get rid of was her dining table and chairs. She had kept them for last because, other than the children, they were the only things her husband had ever made. Old Lady Wally couldn't bring herself to part with them, so in the end she gave them to her friends from the Obeah house next door. Although she didn't believe in Obeah herself, she had always felt a little safer by having these people as friends and was tempted to consult them about her future in America. Over the years she knew many well-known people that had paid a lot of money for these same Obeah practitioners to "See Far" on their behalf. What if she didn't like what they saw in her future? She might not want to go America after all. She decided against it.

The long awaited day finally came for her to travel to California. The hired car arrived to take her to the airport and most of the residents of Louisa Row turned out to see her off. As the car drove slowly pass them on the side of the road, Old Lady Wally waved to them, just like she had seen Princess Margaret do during her royal visit. The Old Lady chuckled to herself, "Well look at story. I get a powerful turn out. This even better than a funeral, because I get to know who is them two faced people who ain't show they face."

The Raindrop

*T*he raindrop suddenly condensed awake in the middle of a small white cloud floating aimlessly over the rainforest. It was a strange place to start out life, but then again, the first glimpse of the world after birth is always strange, no matter where you are born.

The raindrop was brand new, as he had never passed through the water cycle before. He naively assumed that the boring life of a raindrop consisted of lying in the soft bosom of a cloud, staring at the endless blue sky above. Those peaceful cloud dreams were soon shattered by the arrival of other drops that kept popping up all around him at regular intervals. The new arrivals did not pay him much attention, but instead gathered in small groups to excitedly discuss the trips they all seemed to have made recently.

He caterpillared himself closer to a particularly large group of drops in order to overhear their conversations and, without realising it, he became an "eavesdrop". Everyone seemed to have fascinating tales to tell about their voyages to a fantastic, dangerous land that was somewhere below the clouds. Since the young drop could not see in that direction, these tales were beyond both his understanding and imagination. However, he still listened intently, sensing that one day he would somehow get his chance to make his own journey.

Some raindrops had made short trips of only a few weeks. They were happy and excitedly looked forward to their next trips. There were also those depressed drops whose trips had lasted many months, in extreme cases, even years. These drops were tired and needed a long rest in their comfortable, cloudy home.

Advice was flying everywhere. Some of it even evaporated before the young drop could grasp it to memory. However, he managed to pick up some important tips, especially from the older drops who spoke more slowly when relating their wild adventures.

Everyone was in agreement that trees should be avoided at all costs.

If you were unlucky enough to fall near their thirsty roots, it could mean a long tedious journey. One veteran raindrop, who had made many journeys, said that he had been absorbed by the roots of a giant tree and it had taken over a year of osmosis for him to work his way up the tall trunk to the leaves and make his escape. Another drop had the misfortune of being swallowed by some large beast and related the horrors of having to go through the time consuming and extremely distasteful perspiration process.

The young raindrop memorised the guidelines for a quick, successful trip. Avoid trees and animals if possible and keep clear of cities and even small centres of population. Try to land in oceans, rivers, or smaller bodies of water, where you could mix with others of your own kind while awaiting your return trip. One particularly clever raindrop insisted that the best place to land was in the shimmering sands of the desert. You could be on your way back to the clouds from there in a matter of a few hours.

By this time millions of raindrops had gathered in the heart of the cloud and more were arriving every minute. The small cloud had become dark grey and the noise of all the drops talking at once had risen to a low rumble. Even though he was inexperienced, the raindrop recognised the electric air of expectancy that had seized the cloud. Their collective voices became thunder and suddenly, with a brilliant flash of light to show them the way, the bottom of the cloud burst open and the raindrops began to fall.

The word "rainfall" could not begin to describe what then took place. This was not a fall, but in fact a celebration of flight and freedom. A heavenly phenomenon especially reserved for birds, bats and raindrops. The wind seemed annoyed at being so rudely awakened by the thunder and in retaliation it buffeted the raindrops mercilessly in the cauldron of its discontent. Breaking free from this turbulence, the raindrop found himself on a slanting course and began to pick up speed.

Not far from him, the trip came to an abrupt end for several drops which crashed on the back of a large black vulture, gliding across their flight path. To his right the sun dodged out of the clouds, and caused a most spectacular arc of blended colours, floating gracefully towards him. This miracle of beauty magically transferred its colours to every drop it touched. Just for a few seconds the raindrop became a precious heavenly jewel that radiated all the colours of the earth.

The eavesdropped tales flashed before him – avoid trees and cities; try to land in water at all costs. However, the problem was that at the speed he was travelling, he couldn't identify any of these things. He was only aware of what appeared to be a vast green carpet speeding towards him. This carpet stretched to the horizon and seemed to be holding one side of the blue dome of the sky to the other. Little did he know that in just a few seconds he would meet the forest that bore his name.

The raindrop slammed into the crown of a tree that towered over the surrounding rainforest canopy. Ricocheting off of the highest branch, it swiped a large, mechanical-looking black ant off a leaf and eventually came to rest in a clump of highly scented blossoms on one of the lower limbs. Pleased with the outcome of the trip so far he was just beginning to enjoy some well-earned relaxation, when he was dislodged by a clumsy, black and yellow bumblebee feeding among the blossoms. He dropped gently on to a long pointed leaf and lay still for a moment in confusion. The shiny surface of the leaf was covered with many roads and after a while he decided to take the well-worn path down its middle. To his surprise he dripped off the end of the leaf and landed with a soft "plop" in the shallow part of a river near its bank.

The raindrop couldn't believe his good fortune to land in a tree overhanging a slow moving river. In the water, surrounded by his own kind, he felt safe for the first time since leaving the clouds. This feeling was short-lived as just then a family of otters playfully careened down the bank of the river and landed on top of him as he floated at the river's edge. A short distance down stream he had another close shave when he was nearly sucked up by the snout of a tapir quenching its thirst. If this was what life was like on the edge, the raindrop decided to take his chances in the middle of the river where the crocodiles and fish posed no danger to him.

The aggressive tropical sun tugged at the dark surface of the sluggish river. For the last few days the raindrop had begun to feel light-headed. This was a sure sign that the time was close for his return trip to the clouds and as he floated in mid-stream, he reflected on the wonders of his first journey. Not many can boast of being part of a rainbow. How fulfilling it was to be welcomed by every living thing on earth. He felt proud to fully understand the importance of a raindrop in the continuing existence of the Universe.

The Politician

*T*his is overdoing it now," declared the woman outside the Silk Cotton Beer Garden in Soesdyke, "dem people from the small islands does come in we country and do whatever dey want fuh do." She was staring at the front page of the *Chronicle* newspaper where there was a photograph of Mr Hilton Gravesande. He was proudly announcing that he had formed his own political party, with him as its leader and presidential candidate, to contest the next elections.

Although Hilton Gravesande had come to Guyana from St Lucia forty years ago as a boy of twelve, he still spoke with the unmistakable accent of his native land. His early years in Guyana were spent working with his uncle on a timber concession in the upper reaches of the Demerara River. It was here that he learnt to make Wallaba paling staves, shingles and fence posts, which were exported to St. Lucia and some of the other small Caribbean islands. Like many of his fellow islanders, he also tried his hand at prospecting for gold and diamonds in various regions of Guyana's rugged interior.

The time came when Hilton heard that a foreign construction company had been granted the contract to build a highway from Soesdyke to Linden and needed workers. He left the interior and got a job as supervisor of the stone crushing plant, for the duration of the road project. Hilton came to live in Soesdyke, married a good woman from the village and settled down to raise a large family.

A few years later, Hilton realised that the highway project was nearing completion and he would lose his job. He had not been able to put aside any savings and knew that for the sake of his family's future, he urgently had to come up with a plan to provide for them. By the time his last week on the job came around he had made his decision. Early one morning when no one else was around, Hilton purposely pushed his left hand into the crushing machine. His hand was badly mangled, resulting in the loss of two of his fingers.

Before the accident, Hilton's record with the company had been excellent and they had no hesitation in awarding him a generous compensation settlement. Faced with this newly manufactured prosperity, he thought of opening a beer garden under his house. But considering the fact that Soesdyke had more beer gardens than kitchen gardens, he decided against it. On Sunday, in the small Catholic church which he attended, he prayed for supreme guidance. His prayers were quickly answered. While he was taking up the collection during the service, a divine vision came to him. He would start his own church in Soesdyke.

Hilton had always been a smooth talker who liked to use big words, so delivering inspirational sermons every Sunday would not be a problem for him. There was no law against starting a new church, but he decided that the name he chose for it would have to sound genuine. Growing up he had always liked the sound of the word "Episcopalian", but he realised that he couldn't use the word in its true sense, as his church would not officially be part of that sect. He had read in a magazine that the Russian church was both "orthodox" and otherwise; and so the Unorthodox Episcopalian Church of Soesdyke was founded.

Over the years Pastor Hilton Gravesande and his church flourished and his flock multiplied a hundredfold. In fact he was such an impressive speaker that he was able to found the Unorthodox Episcopalian Church of Lodge and another branch in Kitty. Hilton then became the Unorthodox Bishop of his three congregations, and spent his time visiting from church to church.

When election year came around, Hilton was amazed by the great number of small parties that mushroomed into the political fray to challenge the well-established ones. He was surprised at the poor calibre of their leaders, who were also their presidential candidates. Hilton had come across a wise quotation which claimed that, "Politics was the only profession for which no preparation is thought necessary." However, these particular presidential candidates had taken this wisdom too literally. He was not knowingly a conceited man, but when he compared himself to the candidates, he couldn't help feeling superior in both intellect and charisma. With hundreds of "Unorthodox" followers to provide him with a solid political base, Hilton Gravesande had so many things going for him, that he decided to run for President of the Cooperative Republic of Guyana.

This is what now upset the woman outside the beer garden in Soesdyke, so she dashed the newspaper to the ground and stormed into the shop saying, "Islander anty-man wid he cut off han, can't even govern he plate of rice. Look, gimme a Banks, I tired of foreign tings." The shopkeeper and most of the residents of Soesdyke agreed with her.

Hilton wanted to choose a meaningful name for his political party. After considering more flamboyant names, he reasoned that the people of Guyana had lived in hope for so many years, that he would settle for the Eternal Hope Party. As a symbol for the EHP he chose the seaside koker at Hope Beach. Hilton was especially proud of the symbolism of his symbol. As President he would be like a koker to the nation, controlling the ebb and flow of the lives of its citizens. The official launching took place at the Dakara Creek Resort Timehri, where the members of his Soesdyke and Georgetown flocks mingled as Hilton regaled them about the true meaning of politics and red water.

Early in his campaign he realised that he had to broaden his appeal in order to gain supporters other than the followers of his church. To this end he held meetings in Essequibo, where he introduced himself as Hilton Alistair Gravesande, whose great, great, great, great ancestor, Laurens Storm Gravesande was the first Governor of Essequibo. This did not particularly impress the people of Essequibo as they had absolutely no idea what he was talking about. Still Hilton felt that it must have had some effect on them as no one questioned how a St Lucian like him could be related to a Dutchman in Guyana.

For the EHP campaigning in Georgetown was more difficult as this was where most of the other parties concentrated their efforts. Hilton knew he could not win the election and resigned himself to the fact that he would not be President of Guyana. His ambition was to beat all of the other small political parties. He wanted them to appreciate that Hilton Alistair Gravesande was a man of considerable substance and stature in the community. This would not only win him the respect he deserved, but help to increase the congregation of the Unorthodox Episcopalian Church.

Once he realised that he couldn't win, Hilton resorted to the age-old political practice of making ridiculous promises that would never have to be kept. Hilton Gravesande, the man of God, crafted the EHP manifesto in such glowing terms, that if it was ever to become a reality, the living conditions in Guyana would be as close to heaven as possible.

Hilton had been a man of the street all his life and knew exactly what most of the voters needed. To the well-worn promises of free education he added free transportation for all schoolchildren to and from school. As a bonus they would all receive a free midday meal with the compliments of the Ministry of Education. In Hilton's government, income tax would no longer concern individuals, but apply only to companies and large businesses with more than ten employees.

The solution to the housing problem was simple. Since Guyana belonged to Guyanese, each person on the voters' list would immediately get a free house-lot. By his calculation, fifty square miles could be set aside to accomplish this, leaving 82,950 square miles of our dear land of Guyana to be auctioned off to foreign investors. Hilton also reasoned that any government which truly represents the interests of the people, should not charge them for any services supplied by a government-owned public utility. He promised that whenever water and electricity were available, they would be supplied free of charge. In that way there would be no more complaints about water shortages or blackouts.

The Everlasting Hope Party became very popular. Wherever it held street-corner meetings, large crowds gathered to hear the latest campaign promises designed to assist poor people. Hilton Gravesande was always on TV taking part in panel discussions and proclaiming the virtues of the EHP manifesto. When questions were put to him, that he could not answer logically, he would revert to his holy teachings by reminding everyone that God will always find a way to help poor people.

Rumours are the offspring of politics and before long a rumour emerged about the EHP. The party's initials were by coincidence the same as a locally manufactured brand of vinegar. This fuelled the rumour that the Everlasting Hope Party was being sponsored and endorsed by the vinegar manufacturing company. This was not true, and was vehemently denied by Hilton. However, always on the lookout for ways to gain the advantage on his opponents, the EHP vinegar connection gave him an idea.

The upcoming General Election was due to take place a week before Christmas and this would be the time when housewives needed vinegar to prepare their garlic pork and other holiday dishes. Hilton's plan was to give each member of his party a free bottle of vinegar as an incentive for more voters to join. This meant that while the other parties were playing the 'race card', Hilton Gravesande would once again demonstrate his uniqueness among political leaders, by playing the 'vinegar card'.

By the end of the campaign, the EHP became known as the housewives' party. Hilton was proud of this, as he had always noticed that women were especially attracted to him. He had now attracted so many supporters that he felt that he would achieve his goal of defeating all of the smaller parties. Hilton did nothing without a good reason and in keeping with his party's "Housewife" identity he chose the corner in front of the Carnegie School of Home Economics for the site of the EHP's closing rally, on the eve of the elections.

The morning after the election Hilton Gravesande awoke from a dream-full sleep to find that even his most whispered prayers had been answered. The results were out. Not only had he defeated all of the smaller parties, but other than the two major parties, the EHP was the only party to win a seat in Parliament. In the midst of his jubilation it took him some time to realise that the two main parties had gained the same amount of seats, while he had gained the only other seat that was left. The EHP and Hilton Gravesande therefore held the balance of political power.

Hilton Gravesande sat in front of the television, not seeing or hearing anything. In fact all he was feeling was the unmistakable rush of power that fuels all politicians, the power of victory, the power of achieving high office, and most potent of all, the power over the life and destiny of his fellow man. Very few are immune to this intoxication, and Hilton was definitely not one of them.

He knew it wouldn't be long before the phone would ring and those that had scoffed at him during the election campaign would be begging his allegiance. He knew he would not be offered the Presidency or the Prime Minister's job, but he would definitely have to be a senior Minister. Just then the phone rang it was the leader of one of the major political parties, who had particularly belittled him during the campaign. He was offering Hilton the portfolio of Minister of Education and after posturing for a while, he graciously accepted this appointment.

There was a momentous victory rally for the newly formed government at the Kitty Market Square and the members of the Unorthodox Episcopalian church were in full attendance to cheer for their distinguished leader. Hilton Alistair Gravesande sat, bursting with pride on the raised platform with the president and the other ministers. They were all introduced to the crowd and when Hilton rose to take his turn, the applause was deafening. His supporters surged forward to get closer to their leader chanting, Hilton, Hilton, Hilton... It was then he noticed the writing on the placards they carried.

Hilton smiled as he read the first one which declared, "Hilton, the Pope of Poor People". The next one however brought his political future crashing down around him. It said simply, "Hilton Will Set School Children FREE". Hilton Gravesande quickly sat down and as the cheers died away, his outrageous campaign promises of "Freeness" for all school children, came suddenly to life.

The Short Story Writer

O sric Short was a person so small in stature that his surname seemed to be deliberate. He was definitely not designed to do manual labour and liked to sleep late in the mornings. He was lazy. Constantly reminded of his limited education, Osric had sent out several job applications to companies that all had the word "LIMITED" at the end of their names, but surprisingly to him, he never got any reply from them. He decided to become a security guard because it was one of the few jobs that suited his particular brand of laziness. Like most security guards however, he really wanted to be something else.

Osric's hobby was reading paperback novels. One day, as he was beginning a new book, he noticed from the information on the cover that the book was not only on the *New York Times* best-seller list, but had also sold over a million copies. Osric was not normally prone to sudden flashes of brilliance, but it was immediately clear to him that he should become an author of novels. After lengthy calculations at the back of his security notebook he realised what a great idea this really was. If he were to write a novel that sold a million copies and he made just one dollar on each, he would be a millionaire. He wondered if this would be hard work, but then again, what could be more restful than writing? At that moment Osric Short's writing career was born.

Osric immediately ran into major difficulties. He had heard somewhere that one of these novels took several years to write, even when working full time on it. With a wife and six children to support he definitely could not afford that. By the time he made his first million his family would suffer from "white mouth". It took Osric three weeks of careful thought to find a solution to this problem. He decided that he would write short stories instead of novels and still retain his job as a security guard. He was impressed with the cleverness of his idea.

Short stories could be written quickly, and though there would be no million-dollar lump sum payoff, the more of them he wrote the more money he would make.

No sooner had Osric solved this problem than another even more difficult one appeared. What would he write about? Until now his life had been simple and he was not accustomed to being called upon to solve so many complicated problems in quick succession. However, with the confidence and zeal that only new writers feel, Osric Short was certain that he could solve any problem that an author would have to face.

Maybe the easiest thing to do would be to write his life story, but since nothing exciting had ever happened to him, he decided against it. His life story would be more like a long bedtime story that would surely put people to sleep. Most of the books he read were about the unending struggle between criminals and agencies of law enforcement, the more action the better. These were the kind of stories he would write. His training as a security guard would assist him in this, although in his entire career he had never been forced into action. His short stories would just have to be pure fiction, he reasoned. Osric bought a large hard-covered notebook resembling his security notebook, so that he could write on the job when his supervisor was not around.

He was quite pleased with himself, as over the next four months he had written five short stories. But the most difficult problem yet now loomed on Osric's literary horizon. Before he could earn any money from his stories he first had to get them published. He realised that writing had been the easiest part of his new profession. He now had to overcome the seemingly insurmountable task of raising the funds necessary for the publication of his book of short stories.

In times of financial crisis he always turned to his employers for assistance, but over the years he had exhausted all the acceptable reasons for which loans were usually granted. Now, even a fiction writer of his ability could not come up with anything original enough to get past the personnel officer who was in charge of loans. Osric decided to give truth a chance. He wrote a detailed book-publishing proposal that was his first attempt at non-fiction. Along with the usual letter requesting the loan, Osric enclosed this proposal and copies of his short stories in a large envelope and sent it to the personnel officer for consideration.

Mr Seegobin, the personnel officer, was a seasoned campaigner and when it came to loan applications he thought he had seen everything and knew all the tricks. However, he had never received such a large envelope concerning a loan before, so from the very start he suspected that this one would somehow be special. Osric was high on his list of chronic borrowers, so he opened the envelope eager to face the new challenge. He rudely shook the contents of the envelope on to the desk top, not realising that it represented four months of Osric's literary creativity. After glancing briefly at the other contents he began to read the short stories. The five of them were stapled together in the sequence in which they were written.

The first story entitled "Manhunt", was about a police manhunt for a serial killer, and was five pages long. Osric called the next story "The Trial" as it was about the trial of a serial killer, and consisted of four pages. Then came "The Victim" which was about a victim of a serial killer, and this was one page shorter than the previous story. The fourth story was "The Juror", about a juror from a trial of a serial killer, and this story kept to the same diminishing format. Last and definitely least, was "The Sentence", about the sentencing of a serial killer, and this was only a paragraph long.

What puzzled and amused Mr Seegobin most was the uniformity of the diminishing length of these stories. He had read many short stories over the years, but this was definitely a novel approach to this genre. To him it appeared as if the author was somehow battery operated, and as his batteries lost power, the stories became shorter and shorter. The personnel officer wondered what would have happened if Osric had tried to write two more stories in the same series. Would they have contained just a few lines or maybe have disappeared altogether? He had to find out. As regards the contents and plots of these stories, it seemed as if one of the novels, which Osric usually read, had exploded and he had tried to pick up some of the pieces and form stories with them. His main problem was that these pieces often did not fit together.

The personnel officer summoned Osric Short who immediately misread Mr Seegobin's pleasant smile to mean that his application had been successful. He had never been offered a smile or a seat in the personnel officer's office before. The loan was definitely on he thought.

"I enjoyed reading your short stories Osric," Mr Seegobin began, "but aren't they a little short?"

"Well sir, they are short stories you know, short and sweet," Osric replied.

"However, there is one small problem," continued Mr Seegobin," you see, five stories are really too few for a proper book of short stories. Do you think that you could possibly write two more?"

Angela

The sparse border outpost of Orinduik sat on the bank of the Ireng River, as though it had nothing better to do than watch the dark currents foam and play over the terraces of jasper that were Orinduik Falls. The faces of the burnished red rock seemed to bleed from the incessant pounding of the river, as it rushed forward to meet the new challenges of its serpentine valley.

Angela Correia stood on the hill in front of her shop and with sovereign gaze, surveyed the small group of houses with their picturesque backdrop of the grass-covered hills of the North Pakaraima Mountains. It was not a place you would expect to find royalty, but even at first glance, there was no mistaking the pedigree of her bearing. She was the undisputed Queen of Orinduik.

In recent weeks, Angela's thoughts had drifted with the rain clouds towards the north-west and Venezuela, where her adopted son, Clement, now lived. It was because of Clement that her life had been transformed into one long exciting adventure, played out on the frontier between Guyana and Brazil. As her life now came to a close, Angela wanted her son near to her. Her wonderful memories needed to be properly sorted and prepared to be passed on to the next generation.

Angela Correia's birth coincided with that of the twentieth century. It was a genteel era in British Guiana, a time of top hats and horse-drawn carriages, bonnets and parasols, when people were either ladies or gentlemen.

Several years before her birth, Angela's parents, who were of upper-class merchant stock, had migrated to the British colony from the Portuguese island of Madeira. Mr Correia, Angela's father, was an impressive gentleman with a luxuriant handlebar moustache and tangled eyebrows that leapt from one eye to the other without a pause. Whenever he spoke this facial hair moved in unison. It didn't take long for Mr Correia to establish himself as one of the leading businessmen in the colony and earn the respect of the high-ranking officials of the colonial government.

Eventually, the place of the Correia family in high society was secured when Mr Correia was befriended by the Governor himself. His Excellency had developed a craving for the best Madeira port, which was readily provided from the Correia's famous wine cellar. The distinguished gentleman was not aware that the fine Madeira wine, which he consumed in such copious quantities, was manufactured in the garage of the Correia's residence in the Stabroek ward of the city. It was then put into old, dusty bottles from Madeira, sealed with wax and stamped with the impressive family crest.

The Assembly Rooms were the cultural venue of the day and they were used almost every month, on the flimsiest official pretext, to hold a formal ball of some sort. At these functions the Correia family had an open invitation to sit at the Governor's table. As a result, Angela became quite accustomed to "crumbling" with the upper crust of the high society of Georgetown. Her beauty was legendary. It was a unique blend of the classic Scandinavian features of almost pastel-blue eyes and blond hair combined with the more earthy good looks of her Mediterranean heritage. Very few gentlemen of the day were immune to the spell of her charm.

As soon as Angela became of age, in keeping with the old Portuguese tradition, her father arranged for her to marry. The groom was the eldest son of another prominent Portuguese businessman who happened to be one of the richest men in the colony and who also bore the distinguished title of Correia. It didn't seem to matter that both families came from the small island of Madeira and were more than likely not too distant cousins from opposite sides of the mountain.

The wedding was the most extravagant affair ever witnessed in the colony. Wine flowed in such abundance, that in its closing stages the celebrations got out of control and the usually stately Assembly Rooms, became somewhat disassembled. However, as is common with arranged marriages, Angela and her husband were incompatible. To make matters worse he was much older than she was and with his failing health, he could not keep up with Angela, who was usually the "belle of the ball".

During the Second World War, an American Air Force general visited British Guiana and of course a formal ball was held in his honour. At this function Angela and the general were introduced and he was immediately smitten by what he termed to be "the allure of her South American elegance". The general invited her to join his party next day, on a visit to both Kaieteur and Orinduik falls. This pleasant day trip would drastically alter the course of Angela's life forever.

The small amphibious plane nudged aside the last of the small clouds that had wandered close to the endless green of the forest canopy, and began to trace the winding surface of the Potaro River with its shadow. Like some giant ghost clothed in a shroud of shimmering liquid, Kaieteur Falls emerged suddenly from the emerald mist of the surrounding rainforest. The touring party enjoyed this breathtaking miracle of nature for a while and had their lunch of cucumber sandwiches and wine, sitting on a flat rock by the edge of the falls. After they had their fill of food and falls they continued their flight to Orinduik.

The forest reluctantly relinquished its stranglehold on the mountains and allowed the upland savannahs of the North Pakaraimas to unfold in verdant variation. The military aircraft landed on an airstrip of rough red clay that seemed to continue on to the walls of a cluster of small savannah houses, at the end of the runway. This was the outpost of Orinduik on Guyana's border with Brazil.

To their surprise there was a single-engine aircraft parked in front of one of the houses. A group of Amerindians led by Captain Joseff Tesarick, a Yugoslavian pilot, came forward to welcome the touring party. In his arms he held what at first glance seemed to be an Amerindian child, but as the shy child turned towards them there was no mistaking the handsome Slavic features and grey eyes of his father who held him.

Angela's marriage had been childless and as a result she always found herself drawn to small children. This golden child was no exception. In a short while they had wandered off together in the savannah near the edge of the falls, to examine a particularly large grasshopper that he had found.

Long after her return to Georgetown, images of the free-spirited child still haunted Angela, and whenever she met Captain Tesarick at social gatherings in the city she would make lengthy enquires about the boy's welfare. Since there were no schools at Orinduik, when the time came for young Clement Tesarick to attend school, his father

Angela Correia, the Queen of Orinduik

asked Angela if she would care for the child in Georgetown. She readily agreed. Clement Tesarick moved in to the Correia's residence in Carmichael Street bringing a new and intriguing focus to Angela's life. The boy went to a nearby school, and eagerly looked forward to the monthly visits of his father when he came to Georgetown to purchase supplies.

Captain Tesarick had established a network of airstrip shops throughout the Amerindian villages of the North Pakaraima Mountains. Using his small aircraft he supplied these shops with goods, and transported both Brazilian garimpeiros and Guyanese porknockers to their mining locations. Clement's only ambition in life was to follow in his father's footsteps, and after every visit he begged to return to Orinduik with his father. School in Georgetown could not compare to the freedom and adventure of Clement's life in the savannahs. He longed to feel the power of the mountains again, his young legs straining to reach the top, where he felt that if looked hard enough through the cool, limitless, mountain air, he could see the future.

After a long illness, Angela's husband died. Her life now completely revolved around Clement, who by this time she considered to be her son. He had become a teenager and was more determined than ever to be a pilot and one day take over his father's business in the interior. For Clement, however, the winding road of destiny suddenly took a disastrous turn. On a flight near the Brazilian border, his father's plane crashed as a result of bad weather, killing its sole passenger, Captain Joseff Tesarick.

Despite Angela's best efforts, Clement was inconsolable. His dreams had crashed with the plane and he felt that his future had been destroyed. To make matters worse, for the first time in his young life, Clement was now confronted with the illegitimacy of his birth. In the valleys of the Pakaraima Mountains, marriage was not a common occurrence, and most people lived their lives accepting the natural order of relationships. However, the legal settlement of Captain Tesarick's estate was an entirely different matter. After his creditors had been satisfied, the balance of the estate went to the captain's brother, who was considered to be his sole heir. The courts of his Majesty's Colony of British Guiana were not concerned that Clement was Joseff Tesarick's only child, even if he did have his father's grey eyes and dimpled chin. Clement was devastated.

Angela could not come to grips with Clement's heart-rending despair. He became depressed and could see no reason why he should continue his schooling in Georgetown. He no longer wanted to be a pilot. The thought of Clement returning to the interior, where he would not be a part of her life, was too much for Angela to bear. On her husband's death, she had become financially independent and, much to the dismay of her family and friends, Angela made the only decision that would ensure that Clement would be hers forever.

In return for his promise to finish his schooling and become a pilot, Angela purchased Captain Tesarick's entire estate from his brother. With one masterstroke, both Clement and Angela's dreams were guaranteed. The lives of the socialite and the savannah boy would be entwined forever. There was only one serious obstacle that would have to be overcome. It would take at least eight years before Clement could finish school, qualify as a pilot and be ready to assume responsibilities at Orinduik. In the meantime, someone had to keep the business running.

Angela Correia, who had previously spent only one day of her life in the interior of British Guiana, demonstrated her unconditional love for her son, Clement, by abdicating her position as the doyen of Georgetown's social set, and heading for Orinduik. This decision resulted in a total transformation in Angela's everyday life. The woman, who was accustomed to the privileged life of high society in Georgetown, now waited behind the counter of a shop at a remote border outpost. Her clientele was an unruly mixture of Amerindians, porknockers, Brazilian garimperos and interior policemen.

"Correia's Shop" was the brightest spot on the Orinduik landing, a place where cold and hot drinks had different prices, and sugar, rice and flour all cost the same. Angela had a wind-charger, and was, therefore, the only person with the luxury of battery-operated lights and jukebox in the evenings. Although this was great for business, it was extremely stressful for Angela. Whenever porknockers came out from the "backdam" with their gold and diamonds, it was one non-stop party. These celebrations continued until alcohol had bowed the head of the last porknocker, only to begin all over again the next day.

As was expected, fights would frequently erupt with drunken customers sometimes jumping the shop counter in pursuit of Angela when she tried to restore order by turning off the jukebox. She eventually had to learn to deal with what is known as "rum logic". Nothing about this strange behaviour is of course logical in the true sense of the word, but it does have its own peculiar pattern of reasoning. Once Angela had mastered that, she was able to control these all-night celebrations, no matter how raucous and violent they became.

Angela's favourite customers were the Brazilian garimperos. These were rough, desperate men who had spent most of their lives on the frontier between Guyana and Brazil in search of precious minerals. They engaged in the full range of illegal activities, from cattle-rustling to smuggling of various descriptions and usually carried a gun in a holster on their hip. They had a reputation of being shrewd traders who always managed to get the best of any deal. Angela, however, had a distinct advantage, as she had learnt to speak Portuguese from her parents, but kept her fluency in the language a secret from the Brazilians. Whenever the garimperos came into her shop she was able to eavesdrop on their scheming conversations and was usually able to outwit them. One day she overheard them plotting to beat down her price for the saltfish by claiming it had red ants on it. She calmly explained to them that there would be no extra charge for the ants.

Angela quickly learnt that the "Georgetown policeman" and the "interior policeman" were two completely different species. In the city, the importance and influence of a policeman was directly related the seniority of his rank. In the interior, on the other hand, although most of the policemen were usually constables or corporals, they all had considerable power and influence over everyone that lived in their jurisdiction.

The Orinduik Police Station also served as the immigration office, post office, jail and Guyana Airways office. The policemen at this location, therefore, had the power to decide who got ammunition to hunt, who was allowed to cross the border with Brazil, who would receive mail, who would be locked up and by no means least, who would get priority to travel on the overbooked small planes that were the only link to Georgetown.

It wasn't long before Angela had all ranks literally eating out of her hand. She allowed them generous credit for all items in her shop except alcoholic beverages. Each policeman had his own exercise book in which all the details of his shop account were recorded and signed for. In all her years spent at Orinduik, the only problem Angela ever had with the police was when Corporal Alert was alleged to have taken her fattest, peel-necked, fowl cock down to the station for further questioning, and no one had ever seen the fowl again. As usual, the savannah fox got the blame.

The Patamona Indians of the North Pakaraimas became Angela's close friends. She quickly learnt their names and was especially fond of the children. Many of them trekked for miles from their villages to Orinduik, knowing that they would get free sweets whenever they visited Mrs Correia's shop with their parents. Most of the Indians could not speak English, but would spend hours conversing with Angela in Portuguese. She had a special place for them in her heart because they were her son Clement's people.

When the boy finished his schooling in Georgetown, Angela sent him off to flight school in Canada to become a pilot. In just a year, Clement would be home for good. Angela could not believe that the dream around which she had moulded her life for so many years would soon become a reality. She lived for his letters, but had an underlying fear that Clement would be dazzled by the bright lights of Toronto. She felt that he would become too accustomed to life in the big city and not want to return to Orinduik when he finished his studies.

Clement never wavered. He smiled in his sleep as he watched the crystal waterfalls repeatedly dive off of the grass-covered slopes of the North Pakaraimas. He longed to explore again the valleys in the rainy season when he would sometimes ride on horseback through rainbows as they touched the ground. But most of all he dreamt of flying higher than the Harpy Eagle in his own small plane, as he had done many times with his father so long ago.

While he was away, this last part of his dream had slowly drifted out of reach of Angela's financial grasp. She could no longer afford to buy a small aircraft to fulfil Clement's wish to follow in his father's footsteps. Although the years spent as a shopkeeper at Orinduik were happy and exciting for Angela, they were also a financial disaster. The initial purchase of the Tesarick estate and the cost of sending Clement to flight school in Canada had almost exhausted the money her husband had left her. The shop had barely managed to pay her living expenses over the years, with a little left over for emergencies. Angela felt deep disappointment, as if she had somehow lost the last piece of a jigsaw puzzle which she had spent ten years of her life trying to put together.

When the door of the small Guyana Airways aircraft opened, the first passenger to disembark was Captain Clement Tesarick dressed in his full pilot's uniform. As she rushed forward to embrace her son, Angela felt as though her heart would explode with pride. Her tears soaked the shoulder of his white shirt, but she was careful not to dampen the four gold bars that glittered in the sunlight.

After the euphoria of the first few weeks of the homecoming dimmed, both Clement and Angela had to face the harsh reality of their financial dilemma. They were together at last, but the shop alone could not support them and the only alternative was for Clement to get a job as a pilot. Angela could not stand the idea of being separated from her son again. She had rearranged her entire life, and made many sacrifices over the years so that they both could live together in the shadow of his beloved mountains. Although she knew that he had to leave, it did not diminish the sadness a mother feels when having to separate from her only child.

In his mysterious ways, the Lord came to Angela's rescue. The Roman Catholic Diocese in Guyana owned a small aircraft which was used to re-supply the churches scattered across remote locations of the interior. The priest that usually flew this plane had been recalled to England and Clement got the job as its pilot. This meant that every few weeks he would have to visit the parish of the North Pakaraimas and would therefore be able to spend time with Angela. He quickly became a celebrity as he was the first person of Amerindian blood to become a pilot in Guyana. His people regarded him with an awe usually reserved for high-ranking Government Officials and wherever he landed the normally shy Amerindians came forward in large numbers to shake his hand.

When Guyana became independent, many of the Rupununi cattle ranchers had already occupied their homesteads for three generations. The government then notified them that they would no longer be granted long-term leases for the land they occupied. Faced with potential eviction and the loss of their property and livelihood, the Rupununi Uprising was born.

It was ironic that the Amerindians whose ancestors had inhabited these savannahs peacefully for hundreds of years were now enlisted by the ranchers to fight for the land. To these indigenous people, land was not something to be owned by anyone, but simply a gift from the great father of all people. It therefore not only belonged to all people but to the animals and trees as well.

As the pilot of the only aircraft based in the region, Clement Tesarick's allegiance was crucial to the success of the uprising. He was aware of the life-changing decision before him. If he decided to join the fight it would surely have serious repercussions for his mother, Angela, at Orinduik. As he often did in times of crisis, Clement wondered what his father, Captain Joseff Tesarick, would do. Unknown to Angela and the church, Clement decided to go with his people. After all, the only thing the government of Guyana had ever done for him was to confirm the illegitimacy of his birth, during the settlement of his father's estate. He had never forgiven them for that.

Angela had not heard from her son in over a month and her waking hours were consumed by an unending litany of unanswered questions. Had he been a victim of a serious accident? Was he in some kind of trouble? Or was he just a young man busy making his own way through life? Was she just an old woman on a hill, so easy to forget? Then Angela Correia's world came crashing down. She was notified about the unsuccessful Rupununi Uprising and the important role that Clement had played in it. Somewhere deep inside, Angela instantly knew that the illusive dream of her living happily ever after, united with her son, Clement, was finally over. Mothers shed different tears than those who are childless. Angela locked herself in the darkness of her shop to confront the reality of her shattered dream. Two days later, an old broken woman emerged to grapple with an existence that was now without meaning or reason.

As a result of Clement's participation in the uprising, Angela was considered a security risk and the government wanted to remove her from the border outpost at Orinduik. She, however, still had friends in high places in Georgetown. Through their intervention she was allowed to stay on condition that she and Clement maintained no contact with one another. After the failed insurrection Angela learned that Clement had gone to live in Caracas, Venezuela. For too many years, her life was reduced to an exchange of smuggled letters of anguish and frustration.

One day she suddenly realised that next Friday was her birthday. She couldn't quite remember how old she was, but guessed she would be somewhere in her eighties. Angela Correia thought of the first day she had set foot on the grassed-covered mountains of the Pakaraimas. She saw again the golden child in his father's arms. She now stood alone on the hill near her shop, with the cool mountain breeze ruffling her long, grey hair. Angela thought of Clement again and the salt of her tears mingled with the first, fresh raindrops that announced the savannah storm hurrying down the mountainside to meet her.

The Peer Tree

When I was a boy on the island of Wakenaam in the Essequibo River, my father never missed an opportunity to warn me of matters concerning the police and law-breaking. "The courts are not a place for decent people," he would declare in his most sombre tones. In my young mind I wondered if this indecency extended to lawyers and judges as well, but was never rude enough to ask. During my life on Wakenaam I had no difficulty keeping to "the straight and narrow" as my father insisted, because all the paths on the island fell into either one or the other of these two categories. Georgetown, however, was a different bunch of banana skins altogether. In the city if you slipped you never stopped sliding.

After I left school I came to the city to seek my fortune and secured a job as a security guard soon after I arrived. It was at a small dry goods store belonging to a friend of my father, located on Regent Street, which was one of the more slippery streets in Georgetown. It offered a gourmet's feast of temptations to suit every palate and inclination. To a young man from Wakenaam Island it could just as well have been New York.

Women overflowed from every opening. Out of the mouths of stores streamed a tasty mixture of shopping housewives and young female store clerks. From my vantage point in front of the store where I worked, I was caught in a relentless flow of this scented tide of womanhood.

As a result of my strict upbringing, my youth had not been wasted in the pursuit of the fairer sex or, for that matter, sex in general. This should not be interpreted as an insult to the daughters of Wakenaam, but a special tribute to my domineering parents. I had always been an average person, of average height, average good looks and average personality, but it now seemed that what passed for average on Wakenaam was rated far above that in Georgetown. I could not understand it at first, but after careful analysis, I realised that what attracted city women to me was probably some inbred rural handsomeness or mangrove masculinity. However, just as I was recovering from this unexpected flattery and had decided to leap feet first into this pool of pleasure, I received the summons.

I had been in my usual position, keeping an eye on things at the front of the store, when a marshal of the High Court came straight up to me, asked me my name, handed me an envelope and disappeared into the lunchtime Regent Street crowd from which he had appeared a few seconds earlier. In total shock I stood, envelope in trembling hand, staring at the official markings of the High Court that were on the front of it.

My mind raced over the past six months that I had spent in Georgetown trying in vain to discover some incident that would warrant a summons from the highest court in the land. I extended this mental investigation to my years spent on Wakenaam, but the only incident of a slightly criminal nature that came to mind was when my cousin and I were caught stealing mangoes by the rum shop owner.

It was common knowledge that the sweetest mangoes in the whole of Essequibo came from the massive tree at the back of Mr Saywack's Rum Shop, near the outhouse. It was mango season and the tree made sure that there was enough for everyone, so what we did was not really stealing in the strict sense of the law.

I had argued with my cousin that it was not advisable to carry out our raid on a moonlight night, but he had heard that a market vendor had purchased the crop from Mr Saywack and would be coming to pick all the "turning" mangoes next morning. As a compromise we had decided to wait until fore-day morning to make our move, when the moon grew tired and disappeared from the sky. This turned out to be a grave mistake. In the early hours of the morning before day clean, bowels usually start to "boil up", especially when mixed with a heavy dose of High Wine consumed the night before. So when Rumel Saywack hurried from the back of his shop that fateful morning, on his urgent mission of disposal, he caught the two mango thieves by complete surprise.

I can still see the expression on my father's face as he stood before me shaking his head in disappointment. I remember, word for word, the inevitable lecture on the downward spiral of a life of crime. How the stealing of mangoes would eventually lead to fowls, which would in turn lead to zinc sheets and finally to money, the ultimate disgrace. Like all his admonitions of this nature over the years he ended this one with the sentence, "The courts are not a place for decent people."

I found it hard to believe that I could be charged for mango stealing, almost ten years after the crime had been committed. The next day I asked for time off from my job and journeyed to Wakenaam with the unopened summons, to consult with my father.

Everyone was overjoyed to see me. 'Hairless', my mangy pet dog, bounded towards me barking loudly as I came through the gate. This caused the turkey, which was in charge of the yard to gobble in annoyance as it displayed its iridescent tail feathers, like a miniature contestant in the Mashramani costume competition. A deluge of familiar, forgotten sights and sounds that had been part of my daily life for so long overwhelmed me. My family all rushed forward to greet me at the same time, but as I embraced my father, my nostalgic adventures came to an abrupt end. Everyone was silent when I presented my father with the High Court summons that had been slightly crumpled by my family's affection.

After regarding the envelope with suspicion for a moment, my father tore it open and unravelled the contents and its message. With distinct pride he then announced that I had been summoned to jury duty at the upcoming High Court sessions. Totally confused I asked for an explanation, and he proceeded to outline the workings of the High Court in minute detail. Most of the system was easy to grasp, but the meaning of my father's announcement that according to the constitution, "we were all entitled to a fair trial by a jury of our peers", completely eluded me. By this time, however, I was so glad to be free of all criminal suspicion that I decided not to get into too much jury details. On the slow ferry ride to Parika I tried in vain to figure out the meaning of "a jury of peers". I could not decide whether it was meant to be "pears" or "pairs". The term "pairs" made more sense, but with the date of my High Court appointment fast approaching, I would soon find out the truth.

I had always thought that the High Court is the most beautiful historical building in Georgetown, but as I entered the stairwell at the Croal Street end of the building, I was immediately assaulted by the smell of stale urine. After this disappointment, the breezy corridor and it's adjacent courtrooms were trying their best to restore my faith in the institution, when I was directed to an unruly group of people standing along the railing of the corridor. It suddenly dawned on me that these were the potential members of the jury and must be the legendary "peers" that I had heard so much about.

The group of prospective jurors was herded into a vacant courtroom where we received our instructions as to how the jury selection process was to be conducted. As we sat there under the high, ornate ceiling listening to the marshal, it seemed that all the gravity and traditions of the distinguished legal system were bearing down on our shoulders. After all, wasn't this the place where reputations were made or broken? Where lies and litigation were given equal hearing and wills were unwillingly settled against the will of the deceased? Where life and death were dispensed with an even hand? The most amazing thing was that all of these important matters were decided by ordinary people from places like Wakenaam. I tried to imagine what kind of misguided man could have invented such an irresponsible system in the first place.

The selection of the jury for the first case began and after much argument by the attorneys, my name was called. With a mixture of fear and pride I took my seat on the second of two jury benches that were placed one behind the other for this purpose. The other jurors seemed quite relaxed and were talking continuously among themselves until the judge called for silence and the case began.

"The case before us is one of larceny from the person," the judge announced. "It is alleged that on the morning of the 13th of May, 1968, at approximately 10.15 am, the accused, Michael Smart, of no fixed place of abode, forcibly relieved Pertamber Persram, of lot 16, Bush Lot, West Coast Berbice, of seventy-three thousand, six hundred and forty-eight dollars, in Carmichael Street in the vicinity of Bishop's High School."

In our initial briefing the members of the jury were told that if we didn't understand any part of the proceedings during the trial, we could ask for clarification. Both lawyers and the judge were using a language that was unfamiliar to the majority of the jury and I wondered if they didn't realise it or if it was purposefully done to separate the learned from the unlearned. A dry, ropey woman juror who had already mentioned several times that she lived in Lamaha Gardens and was trying her best to imitate the judge's way of speaking, raised her hand and asked for the charge to be repeated. Showing visible signs of frustration, the judge recited a much shorter version of the charges, which he should have done in the first place. The prosecutor then rose to his feet with much swishing of his gown, which looked as though he had borrowed it from a much larger colleague for the occasion, and began his arguments.

"On May the 13th, 1968, Mr Pertamber Persram, a rice farmer, had made the trip to the city to buy spares for his Rice Combine. He was on the walkway between the dual carriageway of Carmichael Street, proceeding in a southerly direction in the vicinity of Bishop's High School, when the incident occurred. At approximately 10.15 am on the said day, he was viciously attacked by the accused and relieved of seventy-three thousand, six hundred and forty-eight dollars, which he had concealed on his person."

I had very limited knowledge of the city and was not familiar with the location that was being described. However, I had read in the newspapers once that some jury had visited the scene of the crime and I hoped that this case would follow a similar pattern.

"Unfortunately for the accused," the prosecutor droned on, "in his haste to leave the scene of the crime he bumped into, and was apprehended by, Corporal Lancelot Armstrong, an off-duty policeman, who was standing on the eastern carriageway of Carmichael Street at the said time. It is an open and shut case and the prosecution will call Mr Persram as its first witness."

Mr Persram appeared to be at least in his early eighties with skin the texture of the bark of a coconut tree and fibrous grey hair to match, sprouting from his ears. The judge addressed him as he took the witness stand, "Mr Persram, what is your religious persuasion; in other words, to what religion do you subscribe?"

Mr Persram thought carefully for a few moments and declared in a loud voice, "Yes, your Hona, is E choke me," and pointed to the accused standing in the dock. The judge made several futile attempts at rephrasing his initial question, but the altitude of his language was beyond the reach of the witness. He eventually summoned an East Indian marshal of the court and asked him to intervene.

"You ah Hindu or ah Muslim?" asked the marshal.

"Hindu," replied the old man and was duly sworn in on the Gita. The witness recounted the robbery in vivid detail, even using sound effects.

The defence council asked Mr Persram, "If you were choked from behind as you have stated, and given the advancing state of your age and the declining state of your eyesight, are you positive that this is the man that violated you?"

Mr Persram simply mumbled over and over, "Dat is de teif dat choke me."

The next witness, Corporal Armstrong, then quickly explained the details of the arrest of Michael Smart and the prosecution rested its case.

The members of the jury were already murmuring among themselves about the guilt of the accused, saying that he was too smart for his own good and that the jail was built for people like him, when the defence opened and shut its case with Michael Smart, the accused, as its sole witness.

The star witness began, "Your Hona, this is an unmistakable case of mistaken identity," he said attempting to match his lawyer's language.

"I have fore-knowledge of Corporal Armstrong as he uses to tackle my big sister, Wavney. Yuh see, the problem is dat Wavney is too big for him and, bad lucky for me, she asked me to explain this to the hard ears corporal. I met him a few weeks back and inform he dat my sister looking for 'big bucks', and no payless, starvin police like he could make it wid she. The corporal then cuff me on me neck and tell me that when he catch me on the road he is going to get me lock up. When I hear the old man shout and look back to see what happen, the corporal arrest me and tell me that he always keeps his promises."

With no questions from the prosecution, the defence rested its case.

When the Judge gave the jury its instructions he was at his learned best.

"Your deliberations must be confined to the parameters imposed by the evidence actually presented to you during the course of this trial," he pronounced with an accusing glare. "The outcome of this case hinges on the believability of the testimonies of the accused and the two eye witnesses. I wish you wisdom and speed in your deliberations," he concluded.

We filed into a dismal room with dingy walls and a tired florescent light that was darkening at both ends of the tube. A long table with unmatched chairs were the only tools with which we were provided to assist us in our grave task, so we took our seats and the foreman led off the discussion. "All who say guilty raise your hands." I was in severe shock as only six people, including myself, raised their hands. The others, most of whom had vowed to "loss away" Mr Smart in jail, voted not guilty. The foreman then informed us that there was no need for us to hurry because we were all entitled to a free lunch, which would be served at twelve, and it was now only half past ten.

For an hour and a half we discussed a wide cross-section of topics that had no direct bearing on the verdict we were trying to reach. We covered the poor salaries paid to the police and the reasons why old people from the country don't trust banks with their money. But there seemed to be one burning question in the mind of everyone. If Wavney was such a "Big One", how come she couldn't afford a better lawyer for her brother? They all agreed that if they could have seen Wavney in person, it would have helped in deciding the case. I thought it was just fastness on their part.

I sat there not thinking of the case at all, but understanding for the first time my father's haunting words, "The courts are not a place for decent people." I wondered where exactly had all these peers come from. "There must be a peer tree near the toilet block in the High Court compound," I chuckled to myself.

A Change of Heart

*T*he Wig and Gown Bar and Lounge on Sheriff Street was a popular "watering hole" for members of the legal profession. Every Saturday afternoon many lawyers and their friends were called to the bar of this institution.

In this environment an Appeal Court Judge and the Director of the Human Rights Association did not seem out of place sitting at a corner table. For many years they had shared a mutual respect and admiration for each other, and as they sat sipping their foreign beers, they debated both the fundamentals and the finer points of local law and its interpretation by the judiciary.

Throughout his career the Judge had taken great pains to build a formidable personal image. He had a reputation for being merciless to those criminals who were unlucky enough to have their cases tried before him. He was feared in criminal circles and was known as the "hanging Judge". Even now, in the twilight of his career, he sat on the court of appeal and dispensed justice to the fullest extent of the law. In fact no one could ever remember him allowing an appeal during his six years on the appellate bench. Just the opposite, in the majority of cases he had voted to increase the penalties handed down by the lower courts.

His friend, the Director of the Human Rights Association, was at the other end of the spectrum when it came to the interpretation of the law and dispensing justice. He believed that criminals were simply misguided people who were themselves victims of their environment and upbringing. Because of these vastly conflicting points of view, whenever they met socially their discussions were always lively, inconclusive, and in the proper judicial tradition, usually resulted in an adjournment for some future date.

On this occasion, however, the discussion began with the fundamentals of the law. "Laws are the greatest inventions of mankind, they are what separate us from the lower forms of animals", proclaimed the Judge. "What about the laws of nature, they apply to every living thing and we would all do well to show more respect for these fundamental laws," the Director of Human Rights began.

"Nonsense! Natural law is for savages; survival of the fittest is just a lot of Darwinian nonsense. For us to have civilisation and be able to live up to our true potential as intelligent human beings, we must have both criminal and civil laws. It is the only way to save mankind from self-destruction," the Judge pontificated. The Director decided to change his strategy. He switched his argument from the laws of nature to the laws of God. "All you ever talk about are your wonderful man-made laws, what about the laws and teachings of God? What about the Ten Commandments?" he ventured.

Although the beers were cold their accumulated effect caused the Judge to become heated. "Our forefathers were quite aware of the laws of God and took some of them into consideration when making our present laws. But surely you didn't expect them to use all ten of the commandments. How could it be against the law to use the Lord's name in vain? How else should we address him when we need his help urgently? Is it practical for you to honour your father and mother, if one is a drug addict and the other has abandoned you? But by far the most confusing of all the commandments are those dealing with covetousness. Far from being a crime, covetousness is usually the parent of ambition. If you covet your neighbour's wife it could simply mean that you are so impressed by her that it is your ambition to try and find some one like her for yourself," the Judge temporarily rested his case.

The Director was far from impressed by the Judge's interpretation of the Ten Commandments and was more vigorous in his reply. "Many of your precious laws completely ignore the moral teachings of God and that is their weakness. 'Vengeance is mine' said the Lord, 'I will repay'. Yet he stills finds it in his heart to repeatedly forgive us our sins and instructs us to forgive others and turn the other cheek".

The Judge greeted this with a high-spirited laugh and said, "With the kinds of guns the boys using these days you don't need to turn the other cheek, one bullet will take care of both cheeks. Furthermore I am quite familiar with the Bible and don't need to hear your self-serving quotes," the Judge scolded.

By this time the Director was beginning to lose his composure. "The arrogance of the law and the judiciary never cease to amaze me. If the Lord in all his wisdom will not judge his children until the last day, who are you to judge them now?" he said raising his voice for emphasis. The Judge glared at the contemptuous man before him and wished that he was in his courtroom where he would have settled this matter without all this fuss. In his most judicial tones he said, "I don't want to hear any more extracts from the good book. As far as I am concerned the Bible is simple hearsay and cannot be submitted in evidence." The Judge ordered two more beers.

The Director could not believe his ears. This amounted to blasphemy, and he wondered if it was an indictable criminal offence. He had had enough of the Judge and his free beers, even though they were imported, and decided to let him know exactly what he thought of both him and his profession. "You display your pomposity as though it were a virtue my friend," he said in a most unfriendly voice, "don't you realise how ridiculous you appear when trying to dispense justice using laws that often contradict themselves."

In the absence of a gavel, the Judge rapped the table top three times with his beer bottle as if to restore order to the debate, and said in a soft, stern voice, "My ignorant friend, the laws of this republic do not contradict themselves." The Director then played his trump card. "Then how come the penalty for breaking the very law against killing our fellow man, is in fact to kill the perpetrator of this crime?" he said with a smile of victory playing on his lips.

The Judge seemed fatigued from listening for too long to the layman's logic of the Director. The poor fellow never had the benefit of studying in London for seven years as he did and was therefore clearly out of his depth when it came to the finer points of the law. As if talking to a child who was a slow learner the Judge said gently, "The death penalty is not about killing the perpetrator of the crime. The rules are clear to everyone before the game of life begins. The law states simply that anyone found guilty of taking another's life, shall be made to forfeit his own in return."

Before a clear winner could be decided upon, the debate was suddenly interrupted by two men who stormed through the open doorway of the bar waving hand-guns. This caused all conversation to immediately cease. A short man with a surprisingly loud voice and cold, merciless eyes, seemed to be in charge of the operation, and took up a position near the table where the Judge and the Director sat. He wasted no time in stating his case as he said, "All we want is some of dat money you all lawyers does teif from poor people. Empty your pockets and put everything on dat table in the middle of the room, and don't forget the jewellery too. Nobody needs to get hurt, after all you all does defend we sometimes. The only ting I sorry bout is dat me en see no judges here, because then I woulda do some sentencing."

The Appeal Court Judge, not three feet from the robber, now realised that fear and beer don't mix well and he experienced some low rumblings below his stomach. He forced himself to relax and for the first time in his life he tried to look as unjudge-like as possible. He was glad that he had decided to wear his Mashramani T-shirt after all, as it made him feel safe from identification in this lawyer line-up. The Director of the Human Rights Association, who always had a tendency to speak when he should be listening, surprised everyone by saying to the gunman, "Listen young fellow, this whole idea of yours seems a bit misguided. If you like I will try to find employment for you and your friend."

The robber interrupted him with a savage blow of his gun to the side of the Director's face and pushed him towards the table where the money and jewellery were being reluctantly deposited. "Shut up, I wants to hear nutting from nobody. Dis is going to be a world record, the first time in history dey got a room full lawyers and nobody talking. Hurry up with we money dey."

As the Director, still groggy from the beer and blow he had received, leant over the table emptying his pockets, one of the lawyers present approached to do the same. In his right pocket he always carried a small gun and he now withdrew it casually, but instead of putting it on the table he opened fire in the direction of the robbers. Pandemonium and bullets rained. The Director who was standing close to the trigger-happy lawyer was caught in the cross fire and was the first to go down.

In the ensuing melee one of the gunmen was shot in the leg and shortly after both men were overpowered and subdued. As the lawyers found their voices again the Judge rushed over to the Director's side as he lay wounded on the floor. He had a gaping hole in his chest through which blood spurted with every heartbeat. The Judge had sentenced many men to death but this was the first time he would witness a man die right before his eyes. He had never given it much thought before and he was surprised at the effect it was having on him.

The face of death was uglier than he had imagined and he was shocked at the quickness of it. Life seemed suddenly cheap and easily wasted, and for the first time he seriously questioned his total commitment to the use of the death penalty in the past. He noticed that his friend was moving his lips feebly as if trying to tell him something. The Judge leaned closer, getting blood on his Mash shirt, and was barely able to hear the Director's dieing plea. "Judge," he stuttered, "promise me that you will try this case." The Judge nodded his agreement and the Director of the Human Rights Association passed from this life with a smile on his face. He knew that the case was in good hands.

A Season for Stealing

*T*he Old Lady bent over and spoke softly to the little Christmas tree in the corner of her small garden. All her children were happily married with families of their own, so she spent most of her time pottering about her garden, conversing with her plants. She enjoyed talking to them because she could tell them anything and they never gave her any backchat like her children used to do. All they gave her in return for her loving care were sweet smelling blooms whose bright colours often attracted hummingbirds. The Old Lady never got tired watching these graceful birds, dressed in costumes of emerald sequins, perform their intricate flower dances.

Butterflies also loved her garden and frolicked on wings that were decorated with the carefree patterns from a child's colouring book. She particularly liked butterflies because they seemed so happy and contented with their lives. The Old Lady had developed a lasting dislike for Kisskadees ever since she had witnessed one of them snatch a butterfly out of the air and devour it. To make matters worse, it was her favourite kind of butterfly, an iridescent jewel of burnt orange that sometimes came to her garden to feed from the heliconias that shared the same colour.

However, as far as the Old Lady was concerned the little Christmas tree was by far the most important thing in her garden. She had nurtured it from a seedling only a few inches high and every year at Christmas she would measure its progress and comment about it in her diary. The Old Lady and the young tree had a very special relationship. With each passing year, as the Christmas tree grew taller, she grew older. She eagerly looked forward to the day when the tree would be tall enough for her to decorate it with lights for the festive season. For her it was a race against time. The Old Lady was afraid that she would become too feeble or even pass away before she could realise her ambition. As a result of this situation, whenever she chatted with the tree, she would encourage it to grow as quickly as possible.

One morning after tending to her garden, she left home to visit a sick friend in nearby Campbellville. It wasn't a long visit and as she returned home the Old Lady noticed that the gate to her yard was open. She was sure that she had locked it before she left but maybe her aging memory was playing tricks on her again. She entered the garden and as always looked towards the little Christmas tree, subconsciously wondering if it had grown since she last saw it.

Where the tree once stood there was now only a freshly dug hole. The Old Lady couldn't believe her eyes. Someone had stolen her pride and joy. She sat down on the damp earth by the side of the hole and began to weep. She was inconsolable. She wondered what kind of person would steal a Christmas tree. It wasn't even Christmas, it was February. What would they do with it? Why did they have to pick on her tree? After a long while with these questions jumbling her mind, the Old Lady went into her house as if in a trance. Over the next two days she lost interest in her plants and was rarely seen in her garden.

Ernest McPhoy was not really a gardener but had worked for several years with a well-established plant nursery. His job entailed both the caring for and selling of plants belonging to his employer. This job did not pay much so he was always looking for other ways to boost his earnings or to "make himself right", as he put it. He did not consider himself to be a thief, but a "middle man", who organised transactions between the owners and the buyers of goods. However, since the owners never received any of the money from these purchases, this in fact made Ernest just a common, garden-variety thief.

During the Christmas season the plant nursery where he worked had done a brisk business selling Christmas trees. Ernest was amazed that so many people were willing to pay six or seven thousand dollars for small Christmas trees in pots. He decided that somehow he would try to get hold of some of these trees and make a quick "turnover" himself. This task was more difficult than he imagined, and it was not until a few months after Christmas that he got a chance to put his plan into effect.

On the way home for lunch one day, as he was passing through Campbellville on his way to Sophia, he noticed a good sized Christmas tree in the garden of a neatly painted white house. Keeping his eyes on the house he approached the gate and rattled it gently. To his relief no dogs came rushing out to greet him. The next day he returned to the house pulling a small cart he had made from a baby's pram he had found discarded by the side of the road. He had always admired the habit that rich people had of depositing their broken items on the parapets along the road to be collected by the garbage man. On his way home from work he often managed to collect things that were quite useful.

He rattled the gate of the yard once again and, after getting no response from man or beast, Earnest walked boldly into the yard. It was a simple matter for him to expertly remove the tree without damaging the roots, as the soil was damp and loose. As Ernest walked down the road towards his home he couldn't help admiring the tree on his cart. It was taller than he had expected and was in excellent condition. It had been well cared for and he was sure that he would get a good price for it.

Ernest requested two days special leave from his workplace and next day, with the cart and tree in tow, he headed for the neighbourhood where wealthy people lived. He was sure he would easily get a sale there for such a fine tree. The problem with trying to sell anything to rich people was that you had to run a gauntlet of pompous servants before you could actually get to speak to the rich people themselves. Even if you got past the security guard and the gardener, there were always a variety of cooks and maids that felt that they had the final say in any transaction on their employer's behalf. However, Ernest was a seasoned campaigner and eagerly looked forward to the battle of wits that was about to begin.

Ernest usually got past the guard and gardener by telling them that the mistress of the house had met him on the road yesterday in her car and told him that she wanted to buy a Christmas tree. She had given him directions to her house and he had therefore come today at her request. This strategy backfired at the first two residences he visited as both owners were away on holiday. Discovering his trick, the guards and gardeners had made fun of him, but to him this was all in a days work.

At the next residence Ernest got as far as the cook. As he came in the yard he had heard the gardener call her Gertrude, so as she came to the kitchen door to greet him he said in his most impressive tones,

"Gertrude, would you tell your mistress that the Christmas tree man is here." She seemed flattered and puzzled at the use of her first name by a total stranger, but quickly regained her composure and said, "Me mistress don't want no tree, Mr Tree Man," but as she spoke she motioned with her hand for him to come closer. With a glance towards the interior of the house, Gertrude whispered, "I got some Christmas tree decorations I thief from me mistress that would match that theifin tree you got dey, you want to buy them?" Ernest was most insulted, "Don't make your eyes and pass me. I look like a man that transacts in stolen property", he asked the cook indignantly, and hastily left the yard.

As Ernest perspired in the hot midday sun, he realised that the "quick turn over" he had hoped for was in fact turning into hard labour. However, he was confident that his string of bad luck and bumptious servants would not last much longer. At the next residence everything was working according to plan and the cook had gone back into the house to fetch her mistress. Ernest practiced his sales pitch in his best English.

To his surprise, instead of the rich owner of the house a uniformed maid appeared. When dealing with maids he always addressed them as "Madam", the very way they had to address their own employers. "Madam, could you ask your mistress to spare a minute so that she could have an opportunity to purchase this Christmas tree?" The maid adjusted her cap, regarded him suspiciously for a few moments, and said, "Wait, is now you trying to sell Christmas tree. Christmas gone long and you like a bad holiday hangover that refuse to go away. Speaking of hangovers, me mistress had a hard night partying last night and she resting. She is not in a mood to hear about trees." Although Ernest knew that maids in uniform were usually the most aggressive, he couldn't believe that better class people would tolerate such ill-mannered servants. After several more disappointing encounters of a similar nature, Ernest returned home defeated.

The next morning he started his rounds all over again in a different neighbourhood, but with the same results. By midday he was still unsuccessful in selling the tree and he noticed that it was beginning to wilt. It did not look as fresh as it had the day before and Ernest began to worry. To make matters worse, just then a reckless minibus forced him and his cart off the road. The cart overturned causing the tree to fall into a trench and break one of its main branches. Ernest retrieved the tree, and after grooming it into the best shape possible under the circumstances, he made a final try at the wealthy neighbourhood.

At the next residence, using all his skill, he manoeuvred past all the employees and at last came face to face with a middle-aged English woman with mauve, plastic curlers in her hair. At last, Ernest thought, someone who spoke the same language as himself. "Madam," he said with an accent of unknown origin, "Coming from England as you do, you are no doubt familiar with traditional after Christmas sales of merchandise. Well I am offering you this opportunity to benefit from my post-Christmas bargains by purchasing a Christmas tree at sale price. The woman became slightly flushed as she replied, "I say, how dare you try to sell me such a rumpled, mildewed specimen of a tree. At this residence we do not collect used merchandise. I would appreciate it if you would remove both your good self and your second-hand relic of Christmas cheer from my premises." With that the prospective buyer turned on her heel and disappeared into her house.

In a state of shock Ernest slowly made his way in the direction of his house. He could not believe that no one wanted to buy his tree. In addition he would lose two days pay from the nursery where he worked. As he trudged homeward he suddenly realised that he was passing the house from which he had stolen the Christmas tree. What a fool he had been for the last two days. It was so clear to him, now, the one person whom he could be sure that needed a Christmas tree was, of course, the very person from whom he had stolen it in the first place.

Ernest gave the tree a last minute brush up, opened the gate and walked up to the small white house. There was an old lady in the garden watering the plants, and as she walked towards him he tried to read the expression on her face. When the Old Lady saw the Christmas tree she recognised it instantly and her heart began to beat smoothly for the first time since that terrible day it had been stolen. She immediately assumed that some good person had found her lost tree and brought it back. However, as she came closer and saw the tattered, withered state of her little Christmas tree she became exceedingly angry. Ernest began in his usual flowery manner, "Good day, Madam, I think that I have just what you need to complete this lovely little garden of yours. As beautiful as it is it won't be complete without a Christmas tree." The Old Lady stood staring at both her tree and the smiling thief next to it who had turned her world up side down. Before she could say anything the man started to speak again. "Please, Madam, for the last two days I have walked miles with my tree trying my best to get it sold, but no one wants to buy it. They have insulted me, called me a thief and even worse things that I cannot repeat in the presence of such a distinguished Lady as yourself."

Struggling to control her anger the Old Lady asked. "Is this really your tree?"

"Yes, Madam, I have raised this tree from a seed that I got from a big Christmas that grows in my yard. Everyone has been telling me that now is the wrong season to be selling Christmas trees, but surely you don't believe that. Would you please buy it from me?"

With that gentle smile that old ladies generally reserve for children when they have been naughty, she said, "My son, in this life everything has its season, even old people and trees. This is my final season it is not a season for stealing Christmas trees. Leave my tree with me and go about your wicked business." Ernest made no reply, just bowed his head in embarrassment and walked slowly out of the yard, leaving both his cart and her tree behind.

The Old Tree

*T*he giant Mora tree groaned in answer to the questions of the high wind over the rainforest. It knew, as all trees do, that in a high wind even big trees must bend or risk being uprooted. In recent months the Old Tree had noticed a growing stiffness in its limbs and a loss of flexibility in its trunk. It had difficulty bending even in the thunderstorms that vented their fury on the Upper Mazaruni district where it lived.

For the first time in its life the Old Tree thought about death. Although trees have the distinction of being among the oldest living things on earth, if it could no longer bend its life would soon be over. As the wind whispered its messages of death through its arthritic branches, the Old Tree reviewed its long eventful life.

The tree had no idea exactly how old it was, but had distinct memories of the major events in its life. It remembered its first glimpse of its rainforest home when it emerged through the rotting vegetation, into the dappled sunlight of the forest floor. As a seedling it was surprised to see so many sibling saplings scattered around the giant, buttressed roots of the mother tree.

Young Mora trees were fairly safe compared to other trees in the forest, which had more succulent leaves. Mora leaves were not part of the diets of the deer and tapir that browsed the area. However, early in its life as a seedling the Old Tree had a dangerous encounter it would never forget. Late one moonlit night a giant armadillo chose to dig its burrow close to where the seedling grew. With its powerful claws it dug a hole about three feet wide, uprooting everything in its path. It was a sad day for small trees as many of them were torn from the earth and flung to their deaths in every direction. The Mora tree had narrowly escaped this uprooting and struggled for survival as it clung precariously to the edge of the armadillo hole.

The Old Tree also remembered the day its mother died. She had many children of different ages, growing in the area around her monstrous roots. It was the end of a particularly heavy rainy season and the mighty Mazaruni River had overflowed its banks and explored the forest for miles in every direction. Late one afternoon a vicious thunderstorm relentlessly harassed the rainforest for several hours.

The mother tree didn't stand a chance. In the already waterlogged conditions, a bolt of lightening split the heart of her massive trunk. With the weird cracking sound that wood makes when it is being torn apart and the loudest explosion ever heard in that part of the rainforest, the giant tree returned to the earth. The Old Tree had never witnessed death before and was surprised at how quickly it was over.

The fall of the mother tree devastated a wide area of surrounding forest, crushing many of her children and creating a gaping hole in the tangled foliage of the forest canopy. The Old Tree, which was about four feet tall at the time, fortunately missed being flattened in this disaster by only two branch lengths. For the first time in its life it was then exposed to blinding sunlight. At first its tender leaves quailed in the direct heat of the sun, but after a short while, the tree grew faster than it ever had before, rushing to fill the opening far above. Its mother's death had given new impetus to its journey to the sun.

The improved access to sunlight also caused problems for the Old Tree. All the plants in the forest clearing began to grow profusely and one tree in particular wrapped its branches around the Old Tree like tentacles. The strangler fig was the most feared tree in the entire rainforest. As it grew its leaves jostled those of the Mora tree for sunlight and its branches tightened their grip around its trunk, slowly cutting off the flow of water from the roots of its host. It was the end of an extremely long dry season and with water already in short supply, the Old Tree found itself locked in a struggle for its life.

Then the fire came. No one knew how it started only that it was the worst forest fire in living memory. It raced through the forest like a hungry Jaguar, consuming the huge mounds of dry leaves on the ground then stood on tiptoe to lick the lowest branches clean. The tough bark of the Mora tree was fire resistant; the strangler fig was not as fortunate. Its thin skin was designed to extract nutrients from host trees and in the searing heat of the blazing forest, its life-giving sap bubbled out of its porous bark. Only the tallest trees survived and the Old Tree was cleansed of its deadly companion.

Strangler fig in action

The Old Tree thought of the exciting day when it was at last tall enough to reach over the other trees and get its first glimpse of the Mazaruni River, winding like a giant anaconda through the rainforest. Far away in the distance the mirror of its ebony waters flashed messages from the sun, which only trees could understand. The Old Tree remembered that just a few years after achieving this milestone, there was the tragedy of the great "Porknocker Shout", when gold miners invaded the Upper Mazaruni, like acoushi ants, levelling everything in their path.

These porknockers seemed to be a brave, reckless breed of people who risked their lives daily in an insatiable quest for gold. Of course trees knew only too well where it was, as they could feel it with their roots. The miners had no respect for the forest and killed many trees to make their camps along the river and to use as firewood. The Old Tree lost many relatives in this destruction.

When they needed to build boats to travel the river, they came to the forest near the Old Tree to look for wood. They discovered that the wood from the buttressed roots of the Mora tree was uniquely suitable for making the sterns of boats, as it didn't split under the pressure of an outboard engine. This was bad news for Mora trees throughout the rainforest. The miners cut large slabs of wood from the buttresses of the Old Tree for their boats and it spent many unstable years afterwards, struggling to keep upright in the squalls that frequented the area.

Day and night for months on end, the miners not only dredged the river, but also dug large pits along its banks. In some places the devastation was so severe that the mighty Mazaruni River was forced to alter its course. It was a terrible time when the river turned to mud and the bloated bodies of dead fish poisoned the water for miles around. Even the animals left the nearby forest in search of clean water. As usual the defenceless trees just watched and waited in silence.

High above the ground where the first branch extended from the trunk of the Old Tree, termites had built their nest. They added to this construction daily until it was like a cumbersome, malignant growth on the smooth trunk. This was a dangerous situation, as termites would eventually weaken the Old Tree.

To make matters worse, the termite nest, which was visible for miles around, attracted most of the woodpeckers in the area and several of them drilled holes in the trunk of the tree, in which they made nests of their own. Eventually, parrots and macaws took over these nesting holes, gnawing the termite eaten wood with their strong, hooked beaks, they widened to holes until that whole section of the tree trunk became hollow. The Old Tree realised that with most of its body weight concentrated in its sprawling branches, which were above these holes in the trunk, it was extremely vulnerable to high winds at that point.

The tree was not afraid of death, but was worried about killing its children when the day came for it to fall. It had to devise a plan to save them. The Old Tree felt that the next rainy season would be its last, as it could not withstand another three months of thunderstorms. All through the dry season it planned and prepared and when the first rainbow touched its branches to signal the change of season, it was ready.

As the rain and its forest socialised, the Old Tree tried its best to suck up as much water as possible and store it in the lower part of its trunk. This caused an even greater loss of flexibility and when at last the thunderstorms came with their high winds, the Old Tree's plan to save its children went in to effect.

Late afternoon storms were usually the most severe, and as the wind and rain came spiralling down the river valley, ricocheting off the mountains on either side, the Old Tree knew its time had come. The relentless wind whipped its great limbs in every direction at once, while its massive trunk stood rigid with water and unmoved by it all. With the appropriate roll of thunder, the squall tore the head off of the trunk of the Old Tree and flung it safely into the forest, far from its children.

The headless trunk of the Old Tree stood proud and defiant in the rain, as a flash of lightning illuminated the two newly-hatched parrots shivering in their uncovered nest.

The Funeral

*H*ilbert was the cause of a serious problem. At just forty-three years old, without a thought for his wife and children, he went and died suddenly. By Hilbert's calculations, he would have lived until he was at least fifty-three and therefore he left no instructions as to how, where or by whom he was to be buried. This was what created the problem that caused all the confusion.

Hilbert and Molly Gonsalves were both born Roman Catholics. However, in recent years, Molly had chosen to be born-again into some new "clap-hand" church founded by a particularly boisterous group of "clappers" from Campbellville. Molly claimed that the focus of the Catholic Church had shifted from religion to the weekly collection at mass. It had strayed from the true interpretation of the Bible and was not strict enough in the enforcement of the Lord's teachings with the faithful. The Church had taken the command out of the Ten Commandments and now left it to its followers to pick and choose which commandments they wanted to obey. Molly felt that the Catholics had made a mockery of religion.

While Molly's transfiguration was taking place, Hilbert had gradually drifted away from the flock. Without Molly to encourage him, Hilbert no longer went to mass on Sundays, but never missed a wedding or a funeral. Whenever he attended a funeral, while sweating in the church full of irregular churchgoers like himself, he would often think about his own funeral. On that occasion Hilbert expected the Catholic cathedral would be packed with his family and friends. Then there would also be the usual "funeral people", who thought it was wrong to miss a funeral once you had heard the death announcement or seen a picture of the deceased in the newspapers.

A good send-off was an important part of life. Hilbert did not want a fancy casket that couldn't fit into the standard size tombs in the burial ground, but he liked lots of flowers. He had always liked flowers, especially orchids, and hoped his funeral would have many wreaths. Hilbert never liked to dress formally and often thought of how his friends would look all dressed up in their "out of style" suits and ties, just to see him off.

But for Hilbert, by far the most important thing would be what the speakers at his funeral had to say about him as a human being. He had always tried to live his life in the proper way, sharing his success with others. He believed that wealth was a gift from God that came with the responsibility of helping those less fortunate. His job often took him to different parts of the interior and he liked to help the poor people that lived there, without any fanfare or recognition. The only reward he needed were the genuine smiles of those that he helped and more than likely would never see again.

Molly had tried her best to get her husband to seek the necessary repentance and join her new church. Hilbert made fun of her requests, saying that he lacked the rhythm and endurance needed for prolonged sessions of clapping. When Hilbert died suddenly everyone was devastated, especially his wife and children. All his relatives had migrated to Toronto, Canada, and embraced the same tradition as Hilbert; they never missed a funeral. Dozens of relatives, many of whom had never been back to Guyana since they left in the early sixties, booked the next flight to the fatherland. It was at this point that what should have been simple funeral arrangements, became somewhat tangled.

Hilbert and his relatives were all Roman Catholic to the bone but Molly, who was in charge of the funeral arrangements, strenuously refused to have anything to do with her former religion. Because of the large crowd that was expected at the service, the Roman Catholic cathedral was the obvious choice. Molly would have none of it and flew into a holy rage. Molly's new found church held their prayer services under a bottom-house in Stone Avenue and that was definitely not an option. Poor Hilbert, who had long ago chosen not to live in Canada because of the cold, now spent an extra week in the freezer of the funeral parlour while the Canadians relatives and Molly haggled over a suitable venue for the funeral service.

Eventually permission was obtained for the use of the Anglican cathedral, as a compromise to both parties. The fact that neither the "buriers" nor the "buried" were Anglican didn't seem to matter to the

Dean of the Cathedral, who was promised a percentage of the considerable funeral collection. The date, time and venue were given proper coverage in all the media and there were to be no wreaths by request, but a collection was taken up for charity instead.

The final day finally came and the crowd that turned up to pay their last respects to Hilbert was far larger than anyone had anticipated. The Anglican cathedral was filled to capacity and the congregation overflowed and cascaded down its front steps. Hilbert would have smiled if he wasn't so cold and stiff. The printed program had to be abandoned as many people whom Hilbert had secretly helped during his lifetime wanted to say a few words of thanks. Molly did not know any of these people and as the Captain of Kanapang Village in the Pakaraimas rose to speak, she was afraid that she was losing control of the proceedings.

The Touchau from the Patamona tribe told the congregation that he had travelled three days to get to Georgetown to have a chance to say farewell to his friend Hilbert, the man who had done so much for his village. Hilbert had supplied what was needed from town to construct a primary school in the village, and had even paid for an airstrip to be built, so that sick people could now receive emergency medical attention in Georgetown. He wished Hilbert an easy trail to the next life and droghers to fetch his many good deeds along the way.

After some other speeches and a few hymns of her own choosing, to everyone's surprise, Molly went up on the altar to deliver the Eulogy to her own husband. No one in the congregation had ever remembered this happening before, but in a calm, clear voice she began by tracing the history of her relationship with Hilbert. They were next-door neighbours while growing up and Molly told many amusing anecdotes of their courtship and eventual marriage. She told how Hilbert had been an excellent provider and a loving, caring husband and father.

Then Molly suddenly changed religious gears.

"But!" she declared loudly, awakening the old lady dozing near the side window, "Hilbert turned his back on the Lord. Although I begged him repeatedly to repent his evil ways and come to Jesus, he refused." The congregation stopped slouching and gave Molly their full attention. "Hilbert made fun of me and said that my religion was too concerned with itself. He said he wasn't worried, that his good works would get him to heaven," Molly gave a great sigh of sadness.

"Hilbert was so wrong," she said, emotion creeping into her voice for the first time, "Good works are not enough to carry you to heaven you must give yourself completely to God and praise him every day. Then and only then will you achieve the kingdom of God".

For the next fifteen minutes Molly rained "fire and brimstone", not only on Hilbert, but on everyone in the cathedral. To conclude her holy harangue, she sealed Hilbert's fate for all eternity. "I am afraid that my husband, Hilbert, made a grave miscalculation; he turned his back on the Lord and then depended on his good works to pull him true. It is too late now; Hilbert can never go to heaven. Let this be a lesson to you all."

As Molly left the altar to return to her seat, it was as if the entire congregation had stopped breathing. The Canadian relatives wanted to stage a walkout and had to be coaxed into remaining in the church.

The Dean of the cathedral started fidgeting and broke the awkward silence. Up to this point he had taken no part in the funeral service, but now he sprang into action. He took his place on the pulpit, cleared his throat three times for emphasis, and proceeded to set the record straight on the attainment of heaven.

"Before today I did not know the deceased, but since I have been introduced to him over the last hour, I have come to know him very well. He was a kind and generous man, who displayed so many humble Christian qualities that it would have been a distinct privilege for me to have been his friend."

The congregation breathed a collective sigh of relief as the Dean concluded his restoration of Hilbert.

"In the world today there are too many who merely speak of Christian principles and too few who actually live them. Hilbert was a man who lived as God intended us all to live and he will surely reap the rewards of the kingdom of God."

People at the back of the church began to clap and Molly thought, "This could never have happened in my church".

The Colour of Hearts

Scrambling hand and foot up the steep-sided ravine, Tobias Van Lang slowly emerged from the damp twilight of the forest-covered valley. Reaching for a sapling by which he could pull himself upright, he disturbed a pile of decaying leaves between the buttresses of a small tree. The uncovered bushmaster lay ready to strike, just inches away from his face. Instinctively, Tobias's body stiffened and even his laboured breathing was instantly extinguished. The only chance he had was to be perfectly still and hope that the coiled, trembling tension before him would eventually subside.

Like a pair of frozen, precious stones the opaque eyes of the snake stared straight ahead straining to detect the slightest tremor in the shapes before it. The graceful flicking movement of its black, forked tongue had a hypnotic effect on Tobias, as the snake tried to sense the odour or body heat of the intruder. He had encountered many bushmasters during his travels in the forest and had once witnessed a man die in agony from the lethal poison of its bite. However, this was different; this was death at point-blank range.

If death must have a colour, Tobias thought, it should be the iridescent copper and black serpentine sequins that glowed before him in the shaft sunlight that had filtered down to the forest floor. The rotting vegetation beneath his left foot began to slip away down the steep hillside where he stood. He gingerly shifted his weight to the other foot, while keeping his head and upper body motionless. The faint rustling caused by this movement broke the spell and the snake eased itself with liquid grace, through the cluttered mass of undergrowth, in the direction of the sound.

It is not often that you are fortunate to literally stare death in the face and have it turn away. This experience drained Tobias of both his energy and his ability to focus on the project that brought him to that particular part of the forest. He slowly dragged himself the last few yards to the crest of the hill and sat down exhausted under a large greenheart.

As often happens after a near-death experience, his thoughts wandered aimlessly through the archives of his memory. Tobias thought of his childhood spent at Pirai Landing, in the Demerara River. As far back as anyone could remember the Van Lang family had lived in the upper reaches of the river and had made their living from the rainforest. What set them apart from the other inhabitants of the area was their vast knowledge of the forest itself. Handed down through generations of Van Langs was the ability to identify hundreds of species of trees, from their leaves and bark, and the knowledge of the uses for which their wood was best suited. They also knew the medicinal value and application of many of the plants found in the forest.

Tobias remembered the riverbank settlement where his day would begin while the forest was still wrapped in the morning's misty embrace and spider webs still wore their necklaces of trembling dewdrops. He would accompany his father and uncles on the long walk to the backdam. Here he learned to make shingles, posts and paling staves from wallaba trees and would sometimes help them cut firewood to fill orders from Georgetown. At first it was hard work, but he soon became an expert axe-man like the rest of his companions, and had more time to enjoy the beauty and solitude of working in the forest. Nature was always full of surprises. Each day Tobias learned new lessons about the forest, until he eventually understood the bond the Van Langs had with the trees to which they had entrusted their destiny.

In recent years, as zinc sheets and chain-link fencing had replaced wooden products, the demand for them began to decline. Eventually, the time came when the Van Langs could no longer make their living as woodcutters and their large family tree was forced to scatter its seeds throughout the interior of Guyana. Most of Tobias's uncles moved away with their families to seek their fortunes as porknockers. As the gold and diamond dredging businesses developed, many of them found employment as divers. His father was the only one left at Pirai Landing, where he kept his family together, still depending on the forest to provide a modest living.

Tobias remembered the day when the boat-captain had given him the bedraggled copy of the *Chronicle* newspaper that would drastically change his life. It had been already two weeks old, but any newspaper was precious in the remote part of the river where they lived. The headline read, "Government Grants 2.5 Million Acre Timber Concession to Korean Giant". Further into the article he learned that a multi-national Korean timber company had been granted a generous lease of a vast tract of Guyana's virgin rainforest. In return it was offering new prosperity to the country's beleaguered forest industry and promising to employ thousands of forest workers. But the thing that particularly interested Tobias was the vacancies for tree-spotters needed to carry out an initial survey of the tree species to be found in the vast concession.

It was almost a year since Tobias and his younger brother had left home to work as tree-spotters for the timber company. They were paid well and were both proud of the fact that they had been able to send large sums of money back home to Pirai Landing, to help supplement their family's meagre existence. At last they were earning a proper living from their beloved forest. This is how Tobias had found himself scrambling out of the creek bottom that particular morning. He was in the midst of a survey of a three thousand acre plot of tangled rainforest, when he had seen death in the face of the bushmaster.

He was overcome by fatigue, both mental and physical, and leaning his back against the trunk of the massive greenheart tree, with a gentle breeze sharing its secrets with the treetops, Tobias fell into a doze. He was tired from his experience that morning and in his fitful sleep he heard a powerful voice that resembled nothing he had ever heard before.

"Why does mankind hate us so, when in return we give them all we have?" it began. Tobias was confused because he wasn't sure if he was dreaming or awake, or if the voice was even speaking to him.

"Why do you hunt us down, so others will know where we are and come to cut and kill us; then drag us through the mud to some far-off place?"

The unknown voice did not echo through the forest, but seemed to reach Tobias through some strange, trembling vibration which he felt.

"Trees have dedicated their lives to the protection of their own ecosystem and the rainforest is particularly committed to the preservation of the entire Universe".

Tobias realised that the sound was coming from the bark of the tree on which he was leaning. It was the voice of the greenheart tree.

"We grasp the precious earth itself and save it from erosion. The very air that you breathe is processed by the presence of forests, so that it can sustain life".

Tobias thought that he had gone mad, because even in the darkest depths of the forest, trees did not talk.

"We provide food and shelter for thousands of species that live in our midst, caring for animal, insect and flower, without distinction", the voice continued.

Tobias wondered if he should try to answer the tree, but decided to listen a while longer to discover the reason for its diatribe.

"We have earned the lasting gratitude and admiration of every living thing, with the exception of man. They are the only animals that seem to be completely out of control, as they continually plan the destruction of the environment in which they live".

Tobias was a man slow to anger, but he resented the criticism that was being levelled at him. He had always loved and respected the forest and was grateful for all it had provided for him and his family over the years. He had never considered himself to be someone who had contributed to its destruction.

The passion of the voice intensified, "The plants of the forest have provided cures for many of the illnesses of mankind, but we can find no cure for his chronic, self-destruction. This has been our ultimate failure".

There were so many questions that Tobias wanted to ask in return, but in his dream he sat enthralled by the tree's one-sided harangue. "Why is it that man lacks the intelligence of trees? Does the difference lie in the colour of our hearts? The heart of a tree is not green out of envy of man's accomplishments, but with sadness at the total irresponsibility and callousness of all red-hearted men towards the universe in which they live".

This time the tree had gone too far, Tobias thought, the time had come for him to speak up and defend himself. Just then he was awakened by something hard that struck him on his shoulder and fell into his lap. He stared in disbelief at the large greenheart seed that lay in front of him. As he looked up at the greenheart tree towering over him, its branches rubbed together and made what sounded like a deep chuckle in the otherwise silent forest.

Tobias Van Lang slowly made his way back to the timber company's campsite near the river. Although he could not free his mind of it, he decided not to tell anyone about his incredible experience in the forest that morning. It was not so much his encounter with the Bushmaster, but the stern, greenheart voice that kept coming back to him. Every single word that was spoken in his dream seemed to have been branded in his memory. For the first time he could imagine what the life of a tree must really be like. The more he thought of what the greenheart tree said, the more reasonable it sounded. He hardly slept that night and by next morning he was convinced that if he identified the species of trees and their locations, then he must be partly to blame for any destruction caused by his employers.

Tobias decided that he could no longer work for the Korean timber company. He tried to explain this to his brother, but he neither believed in dreams nor talking trees. The brothers parted ways and Tobias travelled back to Pirai Landing where he was sure his father would understand. Maybe it did come down to a simple difference in the colour of hearts.

The Bogus Rastafarian

*I*f yuh don't fine wuk soon, yuh gotta move out," his mother yelled as he left the house to play football with his friends. Shaka Jones was in his last term at the North Ruimveldt Multilateral School. After ten years in the secure world of the school system, he now faced eviction from school and home in that order. Unsure of his ability to get a job, Shaka used his last days at school to come up with a strategic plan. His future defied focus and like so many of his classmates he found himself in a serious predicament. He was scared.

Shaka was quite intelligent but all through his school days he was plagued by a reading problem. The words on the pages of books often appeared jumbled and this seriously affected his learning of almost all subjects. The only exception was the craftwork class. When it came to making things Shaka was in a class by himself. He was ambidextrous and in addition had a flair for arts and crafts. Teachers would usually buy the craftwork he made for his class assignments, and would sometimes place orders for special items from Shaka. He decided that this was his calling.

The Guyanese tourist industry was still in its fledgling stages and as a result the market for craftwork was severely limited. Shaka knew he would not only have to specialise, but cater for the local Guyanese market. The Amerindians had already flooded the shops with woven craft of various kinds, including hammocks, grass mats, and baskets. He could not compete with the painters and wood carvers, and didn't fancy the cheap looking ply board maps and other ornaments that many vendors were trying to sell.

Two days before the end of school Shaka announced to his mother that he intended to become a trader in souvenirs dedicated to the honour of Haile Selassie of Ethiopia and the spread of the Rastafarian Movement. "You en no Rasta, so wah stupitness yuh telling me," she replied suspiciously. Although sceptical his mother gave him a three-week stay of eviction to get his new business into production. With the little money he had Shaka bought supplies and began working feverishly to produce an assortment of Rasta paraphernalia.

Shaka had noticed a sudden upsurge in the number of people who had decided to "turn Rasta" and took a gamble that Rasta craftwork would become a hot seller. Red, yellow and green had always been his favourite colours, but now he referred to them as 'heights, gold and green' and featured them in all of the craft he made. When he had accumulated enough items to sell, he set up a makeshift stall on the pavement near the East Coast Mini-Bus Park and began his career as a vendor. All day long there was a continuous stream of passengers on the pavement looking for transportation, and Shaka felt that they could all be potential customers.

In the first week Shaka only made one sale. This was a wristband to a troublesome young boy who claimed he wanted to be a "Rasta" when he grew up. He was so full of the Rastafarian slang that Shaka could barely understand him. There was no shortage of dreadlocked brothers in the city but they completely ignored Shaka and his merchandise. He realised that no genuine Rasta would consider his craftwork legitimate and maybe this was the reason for his lack of sales. In an effort to stave off eviction by his mother Shaka Jones was forced to make a business decision. He would become a temporary Rastafarian.

This conversion was far more difficult than he first imagined. Almost everything about the sect was contrary to Shaka's personal preferences. He didn't smoke and was in fact allergic to smoke of any kind, even incense. His hair was always neatly groomed and he wore the latest fashions, taking great pride in his appearance. Shaka was also a carnivore of the highest order and his favourite was pork. In fact, the only food he didn't really care for was "greens".

After thoroughly examining his dilemma Shaka decided that he would just have to become a "Bogus Rastafarian". Even so, the transformation was difficult as Shaka disliked pretentious people, and the thought of embarking on this charade affected his moral sensibilities. However, he found himself in dire economic circumstances, and the more time he agonised over the decision the more critical his situation became.

Becoming a Rasta seemed like the obvious route to success for a vendor of Rastafarian artefacts. Shaka struggled with his conscience, trying to justify what seemed to be his only course of action. Little did he know that his very name, "Shaka Jones", was, in fact, a pretentious paradox; an unlikely combination of "Shaka", the Zulu war chief, which echoed of his African ancestry, and "Jones", the title of some errant English gentleman who had been posted to the colony of Demerara many years ago and had gone 'native'.

Shaka knitted himself an impressive toque using heights, gold and green wool with a map of Africa silhouetted on the front. He stuffed it with old copies of the *Stabroek News* as this paper was softer than the *Chronicle* and could more easily be shaped to give the impression of Rasta locks. Shaka stopped shaving and bought some loose pants and tye-dye, Indian cotton shirts. He put on one of his bead necklaces with its calabash shell pendant for a final touch of authenticity. Without the effects of marijuana to smooth the edges, the languid, graceful Rastafarian way of moving would call for hours of practice.

After the transformation, Shaka immediately noticed a small rise in sales, though when he tried to rap with his customers, his limited Rasta vocabulary would easily betray him. He would have to do a lot of work in this regard to complete his new image. The role of Rasta grew on Shaka. He enjoyed trying to fool the "Brothers of the Weed" with his acting, and at one time even thought about trying his hand at acting in plays at the Cultural Centre to supplement his income. His mother was not pleased with his appearance, but she was grateful for the small-piece he gave her every Friday without fail. She would come close to him whenever he came home, like a plain-clothes police dog sniffing for weed. Shaka would smile to himself on these occasions, proud to have passed her clandestine drug tests.

He was the eldest of eight fatherless children, and was pleased at last to be able to contribute in a small way to the easing of his mother's suffocating financial burden. The never-ending task of the children's daily care was very stressful for her, and Shaka often wondered why their father had left their mother alone to sort out this hopeless human entanglement that he had helped create. To his young mind it seemed to be just another of life's many complex questions that his father would have to answer for.

As Shaka's business grew he not only took care of his own expenses but also increased his contribution to the family coffers. One of the things he had learned in school was that girlfriends cost money and as a trader of Rasta trinkets he had managed to keep them at a safe distance. However, now that he was a "brethren" of means, he began to appraise the many "daughters" that passed his stall on the pavement daily. Much to his disappointment none of them seemed interested in what he had for sale. In fact, there were very few women that belonged to the Rastafarian sect in general and this was another reason why Shaka found the lifestyle unattractive.

He was intrigued by the small groups of women that passed him on the pavement, usually in deep conversation and totally unaware of his presence. As a result of eavesdropping on these discussions Shaka discovered that they were almost always about their glamorous appearances. They would prattle on about the benefits of their latest diets, or other attempts to improve their shape by loosing weight. Shaka was determined to somehow become a part of this discussion.

After wracking his brains unsuccessfully for weeks to come up with a product that women would want to buy from him, he overheard two women arguing about which one of them weighed more. With no way to settle the argument other than by raising their voices, the fatter one turned suddenly to Shaka and asked, "Who mo t'ick Rasta, me or she?" Shaka recovered quickly from the shock of the enquiry and replied smoothly, "Both of you young ladies are exceedingly shapely, so it is hard to choose."

"Is wa dotishness yuh tellin we," answered the thinner of the two, sucking her teeth loudly, "dis is about t'ickness, meat, na' bout shape!"

"Well I am a Rasta and I really 'ent have no uses for meat, so I can't judge who gat more meat," Shaka continued.

"You gat too much meat pun yuh bones to be a real Rasta, you only mockin' we. Tara gal, leh we go lang." With that the two women disappeared on the crowded pavement.

As a result of this encounter the solution to Shaka's "woman problem" was suddenly revealed to him. He would buy a bathroom scale and convert the part of the pavement in front of his stall into a weigh station, especially for fat women. Shaka immediately purchased a scale, but was worried that with a limit of only two hundred and fifty pounds, it would not be able to handle some of the buxom "daughters" that frequented his stretch of pavement.

Shaka was disappointed at first that all his weighing customers were men. Then in his second week of operation, a group of hefty women descended on his scale and this signalled the beginning of a steady stream of overweight females. Shaka liked to refer to them as his weight-watching clients and he encouraged them to have their weight checked at least once a week while shopping. Business was literally heavy and at twenty dollars a chance, it took him only a month to recover the cost of the scale.

He particularly liked to weigh the really fat women whose waists obstructed their view of the numbers on the scale. These women were at his mercy and for them Shaka's scale became magical. By skilfully adjusting the scale's message Shaka had the power to cause happiness or pain, to grant hope or despair to his obese clients. He would chat with them before the weigh-in and learn of their recent efforts to lose weight, what they wanted the scale to say, and he would oblige accordingly. The popularity of Shaka's magic scale grew beyond his wildest expectations and he became the weight-loss guru of East Coast mini-bus passengers.

Always creative, Shaka invented various diets which he recommended to his clients. They had a choice of the Shaka Sugar Free Sweetness Diet, the Advanced Very Veggie Diet and the Protein Priority for Prettiness Diet. His slogan was "Eat What You Want and Weigh What You Want". In addition he also suggested a number of special exercises, which he had learned at school from a football coach, to go along with these diets.

Shaka's popularity with women and his financial success grew rapidly, and his mother was very proud of him. With his new-found prosperity he was able to solve most of the family's economic problems, but ironically he was the cause of a far greater one. His younger brother, Mandela, who was fourteen years old at the time, idolised him and as a result decided to become a Rasta. The problem was that there was nothing bogus about Mandela. He was already showing signs of becoming a real Rasta and had been caught smoking weed in school.

Shaka became depressed. Although he had not fully embraced the lifestyle, and was in fact a "Bogus Rastafarian", he blamed himself totally for influencing his younger brother. No matter how he tried to reason with him it was no good. Mandela had made his decision and hung out with a group of older boys who were involved in criminal activity in the schoolyard. Marijuana was expensive and they would steal anything that was left unattended and sell it for money to buy "weed".

Instead of Mandela graduating from school Shaka realised it was only a matter of time before he and his friends would graduate to hard-core crime. He thought of his hero, Nelson Mandela who had unknowingly lent his name but not his wisdom to his young brother. What would the great man do in a situation like this? Shaka thought of the undeserved heartbreak this affair would cause his mother. It could even have a life-changing influence on his other siblings. In the environment of the underprivileged, the choice of positive role models is extremely limited, and the authority of a single parent does not extend very far into the tough streets.

Shaka was determined to try his best to undo the damage he had inadvertently caused. Without realising it, ever since he had left school, he had become a father figure to his younger siblings and now he had to assume that role. His first instinct was to beat the marijuana out of Mandela, but although that cure had often been tried by parents before, it had never really been successful. This was time for drastic measures. There was only one solution he could think of and even that had no guarantees.

The "Bogus Rastafarian" decided to give up his carefully crafted Rasta image and return to his former clean-cut self. In some ways it would be easy for him, as he was never really comfortable playing the role of "Ras Shaka". However, he was in danger of losing his thriving business. It was not only his financial independence that was at stake but more importantly the welfare of his family. His contribution had become crucial to their daily existence and most of all he didn't want to disappoint his mother. Nelson Mandela would never live his life pretending to be someone he was not, Shaka thought, as he shaved his beard and prepared for his reconversion.

The Snail Hawk

*T*he soft brilliance of the moon slipped away as dawn crept forward to gently shake the world awake. The young snail hawk standing on the branch of the coconut tree ruffled his feathers in an effort to keep out the nagging early morning drizzle. It was an important week in his life as he had left the nest and taken his first flight. He repeatedly picked at the feathers under his wing where there were still a few bothersome lice left from his long stay in the nest.

This morning the hawk had awakened extra early because his father had promised to take him into the countryside and teach him how to gather food for himself. No more free, nest deliveries, he would have to learn to fend for himself. As its name suggests, the snail hawk's main diet consisted of snails that were found in abundance in the trenches and rice fields throughout the countryside where they lived. The kiskadees had started their usual racket in the guava tree two backyards away. They were loud, annoying birds whose incessant calls had no other purpose than to attract attention to themselves. A hawk would never behave in this way. In fact, kiskadees and hawks seemed somehow to be sworn enemies, and the young hawk had already suffered from their attacks while he was learning to fly. There were quite a few feathers missing from his back and he couldn't understand this unprovoked aggression towards him. He decided to ask his parents about it the next chance he got.

Accompanied by his father the young hawk flew away from the village and into the countryside. To avoid attacks from kiskadees, his father led the way flying just a few feet above the ground until they came to a large rice field. There were no trees around so the young hawk landed on a fencepost overlooking the trench at the side of the field. On this perch he sat like a student in a classroom waiting to be taught one of the most important lessons in life. The harvesting of snails for food is crucial to the existence of every snail hawk and they are ideally equipped to perform this specialised task.

The lesson began with the older hawk climbing swiftly into the sky high above the trench where the young hawk waited. From his vantage point floating effortlessly above, he scanned the water with the smallest movement of his head. Using the exceptional eyesight common to all birds of prey, he spotted the black speck of a snail in the water far below and immediately prepared to attack.

Raising his wings together high above his head the hawk dropped out of the sky with the grace and elegance of a ballet dancer. His orange-coloured talons caused hardly a ripple on the surface of the water as they gently plucked the snail from the trench. With powerful wings beating rapidly the bird easily regained its altitude with the snail held firmly in its grasp.

The young hawk nearly slipped off of its perch with excitement. It was feeding time. However, his father landed on a fencepost nearby and completely ignored him. He proceeded to surgically remove the snail from its shell with his beak that was distinctly hooked for this purpose. Instead of sharing it with the young hawk, as he usually did, he swallowed it whole and immediately flew off to start the process all over again.

At first the young hawk was confused at his father's behaviour. He watched him float effortlessly on the wind currents like some strange, black cross silhouetted against the sky and tried to figure out what was going on. After his father had repeated this routine several times the young hawk realised what he had to do, but he was afraid. He had never come into close contact with water before, but knew that if his wings became waterlogged, he wouldn't be able to fly. He would just have to imitate his father as best he could.

While his father was consuming his fifth snail the young hawk took to the air. Mastering the art of gliding was not easy and it took him quite a while to accomplish this. He kept losing altitude until he learnt how to manipulate the large finger-like feathers at the end of each wing that were necessary for this exercise. He was surprised at how easily he spotted the snails in the trench but his greatest problem would be to judge his descent and avoid crashing into the surface of the water.

The young hawk glided about for a long while before he plucked up enough courage to attempt his first dive. To be on the safe side he

Hawk catching snails

identified a snail near the corner of the trench as his target and tried his best to descend as delicately as he had seen his father do many times before. But with so many other things to concentrate on at the same time he was worried about his aim. His first attempt was a disaster. Like a slightly intoxicated helicopter pilot, the young hawk pitched and weaved his way towards the surface of the trench and at the last minute he made a desperate grab for the snail. His tail feathers became submerged and in a mad scramble to stay airborne he dropped the snail.

After overcoming his initial fear, the young hawk improved his technique with every try, and by the end of a long day he could give a reasonable imitation of his father's snail-gathering performances. It was a damp, dishevelled hawk that led his father homeward in the falling dusk. He was so proud of himself that he hardly noticed the three kiskadees that attacked them along the way. That night the young hawk managed to get his father to explain the origin of the "kiskadee problem" as it has been passed down through generations of snail hawks.

It seems that very long ago there was a severe drought in most parts of the world where snail hawks lived. All the canals and trenches, which provided the snails for the hawks, had dried up. Of all the birds, the snail hawks suffered most and, as a result, many died. Others, faced with starvation, were forced to seek any source of food that was available. They were forced to eat insects, frogs and, in extreme cases, even carrion. Imagine snail hawks, the gourmets among birds of prey, who were accustomed to dining solely on a delicacy like snails, being forced to become scavengers. It was our darkest hour.

During the time of this disaster, it seems that some starving snail hawks were forced to raid the nests of smaller birds, feeding on their eggs and sometimes, even, nestlings. The kiskadees who were the most common of the smaller birds, were hardest hit. Sometimes even small chickens in farmyards were pounced on and eaten. Although this catastrophe took place long ago, even today, hundreds of years later, the smaller birds have never forgotten. Imagine the indignity of such a noble species whose ancestors were once kept as pets by kings, now being referred to as "chicken hawks".

At the time of the famine all small birds, especially kiskadees, had declared a war of attrition against hawks of all species. It was the first known conflict in the natural world to involve any kind of "species-ism" and this had been passed down through countless generations.

Although present-day snail hawks have returned to their exclusive diet of snails, and neither show any aggression towards small birds nor raid their nests, the feud still continues. The young hawk could not believe that this situation would go on forever.

The snail hawks' larger cousins, the eagles, had a simple solution to the problem. They made fun of the hawks for tolerating this continuing disrespect from such small birds. Their plan was to mount a vicious counter attack that would force all smaller species of birds into submission. Snail hawks were unanimous in their disagreement to this declaration of war and 'ethnic cleansing' in the bird kingdom, and had decided to take no part in it. They believed that birds already had enough problems dealing with humans and their habitat destruction. If an all-out war was declared it could most probably lead to the extinction of some species and this must be avoided at all costs. All species must learn to exist together, each in their corner of the natural environment.

This plan for peace throughout the bird world did not find favour with eagles and the other large species of hawks, so tension exists and peace hangs in the balance. Although they are in a minority this does not deter the snail hawks, it only reinforces their opinion of being the most intelligent and cultured of all the birds of prey.

The Strange Tribe

Yuru blended perfectly with his surroundings and seemed to be just another breathing part of the rainforest. Concealed in the thick bush by the side of a creek he watched the water polish each pebble and try in vain to catch the shadow of the dragonfly on its surface.

Eight days before he had left his village of Chilliwang to hunt in order to provide meat for his wife and two small children. Game was scarce close to the village and even as he ventured deeper into the forest, he had only managed to shoot a marudi with his blowpipe and poison darts.

Ever since the howler monkeys had awakened him that morning with their plaintive hymn to the dawn, Yuru sensed that it would be a special day. He had quickly come upon the tracks of a large tapir and followed them to the edge of the creek. From the other signs he found there, it seemed to be the animal's favourite watering hole and so he crouched in wait, blowpipe across his knees, knowing the animal would come. After finding the tracks Yuru became consumed by the thrill of the hunt. It was not only necessary for his existence, but more importantly, it gave an exciting purpose to his life. He already imagined himself returning to his village in triumph, with enough meat for everyone.

At first he wasn't sure if the unfamiliar sound was just another part of his procession of thoughts. As it became louder, Yuru realised that it was not a sound of the forest, as he knew them all. He sniffed the heavy air of the surrounding forest, left his hiding place and slipped like a shadow through the trees in the direction from which the sound was coming.

For the first time in his life Yuru experienced fear, but recognised it only as a compelling urge to immediately leave that part of the forest where he was. However, this fear was neutralised by an overpowering sense of curiosity and he found himself drifting towards the river, which he had identified as the source of the sound.

True hunter that he was, Yuru headed for the riverbank at a place ahead of the sound, concealed himself behind the buttress of a Mora tree and waited. The sound slowly crystallised into a mixture of shouting voices, splashing water and the loud thumping of wood. His heart racing like a cornered animal, Yuru loaded his blowpipe and shifted into a shooting position.

An overloaded boat slowly lurched into view around the bend of the river. It was manned by a crew of five porknockers and contained an assortment of bags and boxes, with a metal drum standing upright in the bow. These men had spent most of their lives travelling on the remote rivers of the hinterland in search of gold and diamonds. Yuru was afraid as he had never seen anyone but Amerindians before and the behaviour of these men puzzled him. They beat the water mercilessly with their paddles as if trying to cause it harm and as a result of this ritual, their clumsy, flat-bottomed boat seemed to be going down instead of forward.

Just opposite where Yuru was hiding, the river narrowed and foamed through a maze of large rocks scattered across its channel. It was not a place that suited a craft full of craftless men and Yuru sensed that he was about to witness a disaster. He thought of retreating before the doomed boat could reach the rapids, but when he would relate the story about this strange tribe of men to his villagers, it would have no ending. They might think that he was a coward.

Yuru couldn't help admiring the crude strength and determination of these men, as with muscles bulging, they forced their boat deep into the bowels of the rapids. It was over in seconds. The bow of the boat became wedged on a submerged rock and turned sideways to the rushing current. Yuru watched in amazement as, with a soft crunch, the boat disintegrated like an ants nest under the savage claws of the anteater.

Only the sound of the churning rapids could be heard as they tried their best to digest the boat and its contents. The bowman was killed instantly as the drum of gasoline crushed him against a rock. The remaining porknockers scrambled around in confusion for a while and eventually edged their way towards the bank of the river where Yuru stood concealed.

All his instincts screamed at him to run, but he stood transfixed by the saga of life and death unfolding before him. The two strongest swimmers managed to catch hold of a tree branch overhanging the river and helped the others to do the same. However, the frail branch could not support the combined weight of the clinging men, who were continually buffeted by the angry river.

The weakest of the men had just managed to grasp the very end of the branch, and after a few minutes, he gave in to the final embrace of the river and disappeared without a struggle. Seeing this, the others renewed their efforts to pull themselves further up the branch towards the safety of the steep bank. These movements almost tore the branch from the trunk of the tree and Yuru knew that it would soon be all over, with these men suffering the same fate as their friends. An unexplainable sadness came over him.

Yuru's father knew this strange tribe of men of many colours and had warned him to avoid them at all costs. He had said that they were cruel and consumed by greed. But worst of all they caused deadly sicknesses, against which the chants and herbs of the Piaiman were powerless. To live around them could mean death. It was no use saving them anyway Yuru thought, as the people of this tribe were not suited to life in the forest and would slowly die if left alone there.

Even though he was scared, Yuru realised that the sadness he now felt was the same as when one of his own people from the village was about to die. Although these men were not of his tribe, deep inside himself some protective animal instinct spurred him into action.

Using his knife, Yuru deftly cut several lengths of bush-rope and knotted them firmly to a stick about two feet long. It took all his courage to show himself for the first time on the bank of the river from where he threw the stick to the nearest man. He looped the vine around a nearby tree and hauled the first two men to safety in this way. The third man was too weak to grasp the life saving stick and without hesitation Yuru crawled down the branch to which he was clinging, grasped his clothing and dragged him to the riverbank. For the first time Yuru noticed that he was a frail, old man.

The survivors all lay face down and semi-conscious in the forest. Yuru melted into the trees and was gone. Without knowing why, he ran as fast as he could in no particular direction, as if someone were chasing him. Crossing the second steep hill he caught the familiar scent of wild hogs on the morning mist rising out of the valley. He quickly found the tracks of a large flock, but it took him over an hour to catch up with them in a deep ravine, feeding on over-ripe plums that littered the forest floor. The hogs were never aware of the shifting shadow of death that operated with his blowpipe in their midst and when the flock moved on, they were five less in number.

Yuru skilfully butchered and salted the meat, loaded it into his warishi, and immediately set off in the direction of his village. After a while he knelt to quench his thirst from a forest pool and was astonished by the reflection he saw there. Distorted by ripples, the image that he saw on the water's surface was not his own, but the face of the old man he had saved, then left to die on the bank of the river.

Yuru could not ignore the sadness and concern that was like an extra weight on his shoulders and he gradually changed his direction and headed back towards the river. By the time he reached the survivors he had worked out a plan for them in his mind. Not having the tools to build a corial, he would make a raft of young cedar logs strapped together with bush-rope. He would give the men one of the wild hogs he had shot and then they could drift with the current, down the river in the direction from which they had come.

As he approached them, Yuru expected to hear voices, but only the forest whispered in its midday tones. The two younger men lay in almost the same position he had left them, in an exhausted sleep. The old man had crawled into the shade of a low bush. He was awake and lay on his back, his body wracked with the unmistakable trembling of malaria fever. Yuru knew nothing of this sickness, as no one in his tribe had ever suffered from it. He mistakenly thought that the old man was shivering because he was still wet and cold from his ordeal in the rapids. He quickly set about making a shelter of palm leaves and next to it he lit a fire. The feeble, old man was lighter than a deer as he lifted him to place him under the shelter on the bed of dried leaves he had prepared.

Yuru felt somehow connected to the old porknocker whom he had snatched from the jaws of the hungry river and was more concerned about him than the others. Filling a folded leaf with water from the river, he held it for the old man who drank thirstily. Over the fire he made a rack of sticks and laid the wild hog meat on it to be smoked.

Yuru used the hours of daylight left to begin cutting the trees for the raft. With only his knife, it was a difficult task that took longer than it should and his loud chopping echoed through the green cathedral of the forest, awakening the sleeping men as if from a nightmare. Yuru returned to the camp and shared some of the smoked meat with the survivors. It is natural to be afraid of what you do not understand and they were not sure how to react to Yuru. He kept disappearing in and out of the forest and they were afraid of him.

Yuru continued to care for the old man, feeding him with small strips of smoked meat. He did not understand why the man still trembled throughout the night, but slept close to him and gave him water whenever he needed it. At that time when the shafts of moonlight reach the forest floor, the old man died. Yuru was confused by his emotions. He was overwhelmed by sadness and lay next to the body of his friend until dawn. In the morning light, he dug a shallow grave in a dry creek bed and with the help of the others, buried the old man.

Using sign language, Yuru and the two surviving porknockers finished building the log raft. He gave them a generous helping of smoked meat and assisted them to launch the raft down the steep bank of the river below the rapids. With jumbled emotions Yuru watched them disappear around the bend from which they had emerged the day before. He then started on his long trek to the village of Chilliwang.

What a story he would have to tell back at the village. He wondered if the members of his tribe would believe him. He couldn't wait to tell his father that the strange tribe was made up of really harmless people. He had seen the trembling face of his old friend several times during his week-long trek to the village and now standing on the hill looking down on the small group of huts in the forest clearing, he thought of him again.

Yuru had awakened that morning sweating, with pains in his muscles and as he came down the last hill towards his village and his family, somewhere deep inside he experienced the first tremble.

In God We Trust

*T*he white ball of feathers exploded on the windshield of the minibus as it careened down the Corentyne highway on the way to New Amsterdam. As I looked back in its wake at the feathers floating gently towards the surface of the road, I was certain that one particular Rosehall fowl-cock would never crow again.

I had travelled to Springlands in search of a steering end for the old Austin Cambridge that was my main source of transportation around Georgetown. It was late afternoon before I found the elusive part, and in my hurry to get back to town I caught the first minibus available.

There was no shortage of potholes in the Corentyne road and it appeared as if our driver wanted to visit each of them individually. Although the minibus seemed to have been reconditioned several times, it was definitely due for another overhaul. This did not bother the driver at all, and as he pushed the tired vehicle beyond its limit, most of the time the countryside was just a blurred landscape. I tried to check the speedometer but the exhausted instrument had long ago given up recording the abuse. Only the tempo of the sound of the flapping plastic that substituted for a side window, gave the passengers any idea of how fast we were really travelling.

I have always wondered why cows and horses prefer to congregate in the middle of roadways where there is no grass. If they were looking for some action, our minibus driver was more than happy to oblige. He treated these groups of large animals as simple obstacle courses and weaved through them with great dexterity, as if a time limit was involved. Pigs and pedestrians were treated with similar disdain, while smaller animals were forced to run for their lives.

When we eventually rolled into the New Amsterdam ferry stelling, both the passengers and the bus seemed to sigh with exhaustion and relief. On the ferry ride across the Berbice River, the earthy odour of mangrove and mudflat was a soothing balm for my frayed nerves. But as the ferry docked at Rosignol, the minibuses all revved their engines and roared up the gangplank single file. The race to Georgetown was on.

Already overloaded, we had no need to stop and pick up passengers in Rosignol, and were off to a flying start. On the smooth roads of West Coast Berbice, the old bus surpassed its previous performances. As we passed through the village of Hopetown, I could not help wondering if it had been named by some frightened minibus passenger. There were several police stations along the way and I was disappointed that we encountered no police harassment of any kind. A roadblock or two with the usual vehicle search for contraband would have provided a welcome respite from the high-speed nightmare that had enveloped us. But as usual the police are never around when you really need harassment.

Instead of looking at the road ahead to try to anticipate our next near-death experience, I decided to distract myself by observing more closely the other potential accident victims that occupied the seats around me. Most of the passengers sat stiffly in their seats with tension clearly etched on their faces and contracted neck muscles. Meanwhile, the driver, conductor, and two drunk men seemed as relaxed as goats in a graveyard. We passed several country cemeteries and I wondered if there was a special section set aside for victims of minibus accidents.

The drunk men were obviously related by blood and spirits and they kept trying to correct one another's behaviour. They were determined to get the conductor to stop the bus in order to buy some more beer. They promised generous supplies of Heineken for both him and the driver. The conductor was willing, but much to my relief, the driver refused to stop. However, our good fortune was short lived as he then explained to the conductor that he was in a hurry and wanted to make two more trips to Rosignol before dark.

A large, broad lady from Manchester village, Corentyne, wearing an even broader straw hat, sat just in front of me. She was juggling a tray of eggs and a small child on her ample lap. At the best of times little children and eggs don't mix, but on a swaying minibus with an overachieving driver, this was truly an acrobatic display. This gifted passenger was definitely left-handed as she managed to catch several eggs before they hit the floor of the bus. However, the child on her right side was not so fortunate. Every time he fell off her knee and under the seat he would let out an irritating high pitched wail. While on one of these tumbling excursions, he discovered a quake of freshly caught crabs that a farmer had stashed under the seat. His mother was just about to investigate his unusually peaceful behaviour when, with a loud scream, he sprang up from the floor with his finger bleeding and shrieked for several miles.

A loud argument erupted between the two drunk men as to exactly where they lived and needed to be dropped off. With the usual unreason that accompanies such events, they kept repeating themselves and filling the bus with Heineken fumes. On a lonely stretch of road in the middle of a coconut estate, one of the men demanded that the bus be stopped and got out on the side of the road. The other drunk man refused to get out of the bus, and kept shouting that it was not the right place for them to disembark. Meanwhile, a swarm of oversized, hairy, coconut mosquitoes invaded the bus to feed on the passengers. Everyone was in an uproar, especially the fat lady, who cracked one of her eggs while defending herself against the bloodthirsty invasion. The conductor eventually pushed the second man out of the bus and we drove off to the applause of the other passengers.

As we neared Georgetown the familiarity of the scenery caused me to be more relaxed and I mistakenly believed that we had experienced all the breathtaking manoeuvres in our driver's vast repertoire. Unfortunately, not being a regular traveller on the East Coast highway, I had never heard of the infamous Liliendaal junction, where many strange accidents usually took place. It was only later that I heard it referred to as the 'Bermuda Triangle' of the East Coast highway. There was even a special signboard that kept count of the accident victims who lost their lives at this spot.

We flashed past the University road at Turkeyen and, with a stiff breeze at its back, the old bus seemed to be trying to outdo itself. We were attempting to overtake another minibus, but as we drew alongside, our driver realised that the driver of the other bus was a good friend of his. The two minibuses sped down the highway side by side while the two school friends chatted with each other above the noise of their straining engines. As we approached the Liliendaal junction the man with the basket of crabs asked to get off at the pumping station. Without the slightest hesitation our driver slammed his breaks. This caused the other minibus to surge ahead as we swerved behind it and dashed for the side of the road.

What happened next seemed to be in slow motion. The front of a Banks DIH truck was trying to force its way through the side window of the minibus nearest to where I sat and I felt the angry heat of its radiator just before impact. Several strange things then happened in no particular sequence.

The conductor let go of the wad of money that he had clutched tightly in his fist since the journey began. At last the fat lady dropped the eggs and scrambled her child. The driver finally stopped his reckless driving and dived for safety among the passengers. I saw sky, then road, then sky, then trench water, as we came to rest in a wide, shallow trench at the side of the road. People were crying and the child was silent. I tasted blood and hoped that it was my own.

After turning over several times, the bus had landed on its side, with the passenger side door buried in the mud. Crabs and passengers slowly crawled out of the front door and windows of the minibus. Miraculously, the conductor and the rest of the passengers all sustained only minor injuries, but it was maybe fitting that the driver had gotten the worst of it. He lay in the bus in a semi-conscious condition and had to be lifted to the side of the road by three of the passengers that were still in good shape.

I was in shock and sat in the grass of the parapet near a red ants nest and watched the ants climb on to my swollen ankle. It has always amazed me how fast ants travel when they are investigating some foreign object that has been suddenly dumped into their lives. As I sat there sipping the mixture of blood and trench water trickling down from a cut on my forehead, I wondered if my ankle was broken and if it would feel when the ants began to bite.

As I mumbled a short prayer of thanksgiving, I glanced at the minibus and noticed for the first time the name stencilled boldly across its side. It proclaimed simply, "IN GOD WE TRUST".

An Immigration Affair

The irritating Canadian voice on the clock radio prised Boysie Chatagoon's eyelids open. It was Saturday. He didn't have to go to work but had forgotten to prevent the alarm from delivering its weekday, wake-up message. The wild party the night before at the Painted Post Disco, now severely hampered his ability to regain consciousness. Although the dimness of a hangover is not the ideal environment for serious reflection, Boysie for some reason felt the need to review his life in Canada.

Boysie's first thought was that his time spent in Toronto had been little more than one extended hangover lasting eight years. He blamed not only his propensity for all-night partying, but his switch from good Guyanese rum to cheap vodka, that was now his drink of necessity, and not of choice. Like most things in Canada, it was colourless.

He thought of his home in No. 63 village on the Corentyne coast in Guyana. Boysie smiled as he remembered the golden rum and women from his village. They both seemed to share sugarcane as the source of their sweetness and their haunting after taste usually created a slow addiction. In that surreal state between sleep and wakefulness, the apartment on the fourteenth floor in Scarborough was transformed into Boysie's beloved seashore, for which his village was famous. A distinct saline fragrance, a blend of mud, crabs and dry coconuts, seemed to flood the apartment like the incoming tide.

When Boysie Chatagoon migrated to Canada as a nineteen-year-old from a remote rural district of the Guyana coastland, he was overwhelmed by the massive city of Toronto. His overloaded senses had difficulty grappling with the extreme contrasts of the big city when compared to his backward village. He was totally unprepared for the shock to his third-world psyche. Boysie felt that he had suddenly been deposited in the middle of the making of one of the exciting movies he sometimes saw at the bug-infested cinema near his village. He felt the responsibility to act out the role he had been given in this big city drama.

Boysie quickly acquired, what was in his opinion, a competent Canadian accent and set about getting acquainted with the hundreds of white women who came towards him daily, from every direction, on the busy streets. His first impression was that Toronto was a bachelor's paradise. However, Canadianisation was far more difficult than it had first appeared, and it took Boysie almost two years to learn to march to this new drummer. For some one in tune with the laidback Caribbean rhythm, the North American beat seemed harsh and impersonal.

Although Boysie considered himself to be a serious student of life, and had a certain highly developed grass roots intelligence to prove it, his lack of formal education severely limited his choices. After many humiliating interviews, he finally got a job at a factory that manufactured Thermos flasks. Boysie found the work easy enough, but it was mentally stifling. The monotony of the assembly line was surpassed only by the dull sameness of his workmates.

Like so many immigrants from Third World countries, Boysie could not accept the reality that in his new life he would be condemned to an almost robotic existence of tending an assembly line. In many ways this job bore an uncanny resemblance to the lifestyle of the average inhabitant of the big city. Like worker bees in some giant hive, they were condemned to a life of endless toil producing honey without ever having the opportunity to sample it. He would just have to do better, Boysie thought.

Boysie Chatagoon heard stories about handsome young men of his own age, who did not have to work at all because they managed to persuade rich middle-aged women to pay all their living expenses. He considered this unbelievable type of sponsored relationship to be the highest form of employment to which a young man could aspire. All the middle-aged Hindu women in Guyana that he knew did not have a cent of their own. Boysie was considered to be one of the most handsome young men in No. 63 village and he saw no reason why he should not cash in on his good looks. He would organise one of these "love for rent" relationships for himself.

Long before it became accepted police procedure, Boysie engaged in profiling. With a rich, middle-aged focus, he approached several potential employers. Much to his surprise, they were all quite indignant at the lewdness of his propositions. Instead of losing heart, Boysie changed his strategy entirely. He decided to pose as a person carrying out an informal, scientific survey on the prevalence of relationships involving gigolos and their sponsors. Armed with an official-looking clipboard, he harassed many middle-aged women who had the misfortune to pass his workplace during his lunch hour. Boysie's impersonation was very unprofessional and his scam was soon discovered. The project came to a serious conclusion when one of his victims reported him to the police. He was arrested, mistaken for a Pakistani and taken down to the station. As a first offender Boysie was released with a severe warning.

However, this experience only made him more aware of the many exciting opportunities that were available in the large cities of North America. Boysie received several propositions to become a courier or salesman for a wide range of illegal drugs. But when he considered the wide range of sentences, which included prison, deportation or even death at a young age, they didn't seem adequate enough compensation for the job. Eventually, Boysie's deliverance from his factory enslavement came by way of his cousin, on a visit from Montreal.

Bal had come to Toronto for the wedding of one of Boysie's relatives and stayed at his apartment for the weekend. In answer to Boysie's enquiries about job opportunities in Montreal, Bal outlined to him an immigration scam in which he was presently participating. It involved a marriage of convenience to a girl from Guyana, in order to make her eligible to live in Canada as the spouse of a landed immigrant. The grateful bride was willing to pay a fee of ten thousand Canadian dollars to the temporary groom as compensation for his pain and suffering during the ordeal. Boysie had found his calling in life. He made contact with the people in charge of the racket in Toronto and offered his matrimonial services.

After only a few weeks, Boysie was informed that a potential bride was available, but he would first have to undergo an important series of prenuptial classes before the contract could be signed. He was amazed at how thorough the arrangements were. Back in Guyana, Zara Ali's father notified her by letter of her matrimonial arrangements and that a husband had been identified for her. Enclosed were three additional pages of information about Boysie Chattergoon that needed to be learned by heart. The groom's favourite colour, food, relative, book and movie, along with a long list of biographical information, designed to answer any question the Canadian Immigration could possibly ask.

When Zara Ali's family had migrated to Canada four years before she had missed the age limit by just a few months. Ever since then, like a convict on death row, Zara had waited alone for her appeal to be granted by the Canadian Government. However, for Zara, there seemed to be no legal reprieve; no happy ending.

The separation of parents in their old age from their children, to whom they have devoted their entire existence, must surely be one of the most undeserved rewards of parenthood. Zara's father, whose heart condition seemed to deteriorate with every heart-rending letter he received from his distraught daughter in Guyana, was forced to resort to desperate measures.

The Alis were a large, close-knit family who, like so many others in Guyana, had been inexorably torn apart by the cruel necessity of migration. Zara Ali thought about her impending arranged marriage and wept. These were not the usual tears of bridal bliss, but the terrified tears of embarking blindly on an unknown voyage. She thought of the unfortunate plight of thousands of young Indian women the world over, who suffered the same fate every day in silent submission. Just when she thought things couldn't get worse she realised that the groom, Boysie Chatagoon, was a Hindu. In the depths of their desperation the Ali family, who were devout Muslims, had managed to overlook even this major obstacle.

As mandated by the marriage agreement, Zara began to receive love letters from a total stranger. In order to be able to reply to them with the same degree of insincere sincerity, Zara tried in vain to conjure up a vision of Boysie Chatagoon's face. His features defied imaginary focus and her letters were complicated by conflicting emotions. The fact that she was sworn to secrecy in the initial stages of the process, made the psychological pressure almost unbearable.

The matrimonial plan recommended that Boysie travel to Guyana to meet his prospective bride after three months of courtship by mail. Zara fantasised that her situation would somehow evolve into a "Cinderella" story. With all her heart she prayed that Boysie would turn out to be her "Prince Charming", and not some ugly stepbrother. She was sorry that she didn't know any Hindu prayers to add to her daily besiegement of Allah on this subject.

When Zara Ali laid eyes on Boysie Chatagoon for the first time at Timehri Airport, she could not believe her good fortune. She raised her eyes to heaven in a quick gesture of thanks to the Holy One for his intervention. Boysie was not only handsome, but had the debonair confidence of a Guyanese returning home from North America. Resplendent in the latest Tommy Hilfiger outfit and top of the line Nike track shoes, he could have been the son of an Indian Maharajah, as far as Zara was concerned. However, Boysie quickly informed Zara that he would be spending the first week of his vacation at his home in No. 63 village and they would only meet again a few days before his departure. With those few, impersonal words, he was gone.

The call of love echoes loudest in an empty heart and for Zara Ali, it was unmistakable. In her imagination, her fears dissolved in the warm positive images of Boysie Chatagoon. She longed for the opportunity to get to know him better.

Boysie's next visit was strictly business. Together they went over their matrimonial arrangements. The engagement was the next phase of the plan and this was scheduled to take place in Guyana, in four months time. A further six months after that, while Zara was on a visit to Toronto, they would get married. Boysie would then apply for an extension of Zara's visitor's visa, under spousal privilege, pending the processing of her permanent papers.

Before he departed, Boysie and Zara took a photograph sitting together on the sea wall holding hands. This photograph had to be displayed prominently in Boysie's Toronto apartment as proof of the progressing love affair. Zara kept hers under her pillow where it could easily be accessed as a source of dreams. The engagement went according to plan and when Zara Ali burst into the welcoming area at the Toronto Airport, her jubilant family was all there to meet her. Hugs and kisses rained like silk cotton seeds when the big tree in their yard in the village was in season. Zara was overjoyed to be reunited with her family at last, after five painful years of separation. But in the midst of her euphoria, somewhere deep inside, there was a nagging blemish of disappointment. On the long drive from the airport she realised it was a blemish that only the sight of Boysie Chatagoon could erase.

The engaged couple met a few days later, and Zara was even more impressed by Boysie's dashing familiarity with the big city environment that was strangely frightening to her. At the same time, however, Boysie Chatagoon was experiencing emotions that were exactly the opposite. His visit to his home at No. 63 village in Guyana had been a personal disaster. The kind brush of nostalgia had painted too flattering a picture on the canvas of his memory. As a result Boysie was disappointed with everything. The scale and sophistication of the village were so different from the big city that it felt almost claustrophobic. He found it hard to accept that, less than ten years before, he himself had been one of these simple, hard-working villagers.

Boysie used to do the back-breaking work of loading punts with sugarcane all day in the cane fields, with the dreaded Corentyne sun as his constant companion. In the evenings he would congregate with his friends on the sea wall near the koker and watch the village women who came to buy fish from the boats moored there. Boysie Chatagoon was not ashamed of his roots, but was now a stranger among familiar things. He could never return to live in Guyana. His life had changed forever. He would now be forced to accept, without complaint, whatever hardships his adopted country imposed upon him. The innocent simplicity of Zara Ali sitting before him, now forced him to focus on those unwanted memories of a Guyana which he had already cast aside.

The wedding was doomed to be a paradox from the outset. For the Alis, it was a joyous celebration of family completion. The final piece of the family mosaic was now in place. In stark contrast, for the Chatagoons, the wedding was the cause of family discord. The fact that Boysie was marrying a Muslim woman was viewed as a desecration of the holy traditions of the Hindu religion and they wanted no part of it.

Early one Saturday morning, with the members of the Ali family as their witnesses, Boysie and Zara were married at City Hall, according to the laws of Canada. During the small reception at the Ali's apartment, the down-payment of five thousand dollars was handed over to the groom as agreed. Boysie Chatagoon had assembled his last Thermos flask. The married couple rented an apartment of their own, in order to create the impression of normal newly-weds. Of course, Boysie kept his old apartment, where he would return late every night to sleep. After all, in his mind, he was still a bachelor and never missed an opportunity to remind Zara of this.

Zara came home every evening exhausted from work and a tedious commute involving two subways and three buses. Like the average Canadian couple she and Boysie sat in front of the television and allowed the magic box to distract them from the seemingly endless monotony of their lives. Zara was quite pleased with the arrangement. After the long years of loneliness spent in Guyana, she was like a parched sponge, eager to absorb even the smallest act of kindness that Boysie accidentally threw her way. She would often misinterpret his courteous remarks or gestures to be the first glimmers of affection. Zara took her domestic duties very seriously and every evening she would prepare spicy Indian dishes that Boysie had not enjoyed since leaving Guyana. It was not difficult for her to please Boysie. She had been supplied with a long list of his favourite things, as part of the immigration scam.

The Ali family could not afford Boysie's fee and Zara's father had to take a loan from the bank. Zara felt personally responsible for this debt, and worked gruelling hours at two jobs to help repay it. She didn't blame Boysie for her modern day indentureship, but instead thought of him as her saviour. She felt that his fee was a reasonable purchase price for her happiness. Zara's Visitors Visa was extended and her application for landed immigrant status began its snail-like journey through the maze of the immigration bureaucracy. Zara may have been the first person to ever cheerfully welcome this lengthy process. The longer it took the more opportunity she would have to transform her marriage from a counterfeit contract into a union of legitimate love.

Zara Ali was extremely happy with her new life. She was amazed at how easily she adjusted to the vast differences in both culture and environment. She was a very likable person and made many friends at both of her workplaces. Timid at first, Zara gradually accepted their invitations to socialise after work, especially on Fridays. Boysie, who had lost his taste for "fast food" as a result of Zara's excellent cooking, was left without dinner with increasing regularity. He thought of complaining to her about this treatment but wasn't sure if it was covered in the contract. Looking at his favourite shows alone was not much fun either. Boysie was surprised at how accustomed he had become to Zara's light-hearted companionship.

The domestic situation for the newly-weds deteriorated even further as Zara was gone all day on weekends. There was so much for her to experience, like trips to Niagara Falls and Marineland. Although she invited him to accompany her, Boysie had seen it all before many times and was not interested in going again. The only thing that was new to him was his change of lifestyle due to his bogus marriage to Zara. Where that was concerned he wasn't sure if he was confusing the taste of her cooking with the taste of settling down. Whatever it was, Boysie realised it was habit-forming. He would have to be very careful.

He noticed that living in Toronto had quickly changed Zara's personality. She was now almost the complete opposite of the nervous, frightened girl, who had avoided making eye contact with him when they met in Guyana. In just a few months she had become sure of herself, had an opinion about almost everything and was not afraid to voice it whenever possible. Boysie sometimes even detected a touch of growing sophistication about her.

Zara Ali's assessment of Boysie was not as kind. She was still very attracted to him, but had come to realise that he lacked the necessary ambition to be successful. Although she was thankful that it had brought her to Canada, the mere fact that he would participate in a marriage for money scheme identified him as a callous opportunist. Zara was afraid that Boysie's distaste for hard work and penchant for easy money, would eventually lead him to a life of more serious crime.

After many months of impersonal, domestic existence in their closely tailored apartment, it happened suddenly one evening. Quite by accident, Zara found herself wrapped tightly in Boysie's arms. Like a sluggish river that meanders a great distance to the edge of an escarpment, then becomes a raging waterfall, Zara Ali threw herself over the emotional precipice. After a year of marriage, the union was consummated.

Instead of simplifying matters, this romantic capitulation transformed the already complex situation into a hopeless tangle of emotions. Zara had never been able to properly assess Boysie's sincerity and always felt that there was some ulterior motive for his actions. For the first time in the relationship she felt that the power had shifted in her favour. She changed her mind about her permanent papers and now hoped that they would come through as soon as possible. Zara reasoned that this would force Boysie to declare his true feelings for her. When the news did come, however, it was of an entirely unexpected nature. Zara Ali was pregnant.

Zara realised that in a few short months her indiscretion would be exposed. During this time, she had so many momentous decisions to make that would drastically impact the future of both her and her unborn child. Zara Ali had no one to confide in. Although she was a legally married woman, she felt as if her child was illegitimate and was ashamed to face her family. Where Boysie was concerned, she just wasn't sure about anything. Funny enough, she felt that Boysie would welcome the news. She knew he loved children, but was he ready to settle down to family life? Zara had her doubts.

Zara's confused deliberations always seemed to return to one basic, overriding question. Could a marriage founded on falsehood ever come true? She felt that at the back of Boysie's mind their marriage would always be a temporary arrangement, and at the first sign of hardship, he would leave without a backward glance. Zara thought of her unborn child of indeterminate religion, and vowed to make its needs her only priority. She begged Allah to make sure her papers came before Boysie discovered her pregnancy. Zara noticed that since meeting Boysie she had developed a particularly close relationship with Allah.

Ever since they had made love the first time, Zara avoided being alone with Boysie. Although he had tried his best to initiate romantic contact between them, she had skilfully managed to limit their intimacies without totally discouraging his advances. This was extremely difficult for Zara. She had sampled the intoxicating brew of wanton desire, for which there can be no substitute. With every passing day Zara Ali's resolve grew weaker.

Just as she was finding it necessary to wear loose fitting clothes in order to disguise her condition, the fateful envelope from the Canadian Immigration arrived. Zara was legal. The next day she collected the five thousand dollars from her father that would complete her payment to Boysie and prepared a romantic dinner for him

After the enjoyable dinner of his favourite dishes, Boysie noticed that Zara was in an unusually receptive mood and soon made amorous advances towards her. With her most alluring smile, Zara Ali casually presented him with his payment in full according to their marriage contract. Boysie was confused. For almost two years he had waited eagerly for this day and now that it had eventually come, it somehow felt indecent.

Boysie knew how much of a sacrifice it was for the Ali family to come up with his fee and it seemed to be an obscene imposition on his part. He looked at the envelope containing the wages of his deception and then at Zara's sweet, contented smile. For the first time in his life Boysie Chatagoon hated himself. He realised that over the last few months he had reluctantly fallen in love with Zara Ali, but had refused to admit it even to himself. Since they had made passionate love together, she had become a fascinating mystery and he was no longer sure of what he should do next. Whatever it was, Boysie was sure the time to do it had come.

He wanted to propose to her, but they were already married. Boysie Chatagoon apologised sincerely for all the anguish he had caused the Ali family. He put the envelope carefully down on the coffee table and threw himself on Zara's lap. She hugged her husband's head to her belly tenderly and whispered the news of their child in his ear. She smiled as she watched their tears mingle and fall on the flowered pattern of her dress where it tightened around her stomach.

Donkey Experience

*A*s a young boy with my feet dangling over the side of my father's dray-cart and stray dogs snapping at the heels of the trotting horse, I knew that this was the life for me. All I wanted was to be a dray-cart man. What a life. It was like drifting through the city streets on a small cloud, chased by the wind. It was a song of freedom accompanied by the intricate percussion of hoof and harness, mingled with the exciting odour of the sweating horse.

When I became a teenager, I mentioned to my father my intention of becoming a cart man and following in his footsteps. He seemed to be both proud and disappointed at the same time. However, this emotional confusion didn't last long as he decided to give me a stern lecture on the finer points of my chosen profession. He explained that working a dray-cart was not an alternative to a good secondary education. Cart men had to be able to make all kinds of serious calculations involving transportation rates, like the cost of grass versus gas for example.

The matter of when I would begin working was settled when my favourite uncle from Golden Grove, having heard of my plans, arrived one Sunday at our home in Campbellville to present me with a donkey. I could not contain my excitement until I went to the back of the yard and saw the small, grey animal tied to the fence. It was old and thin, but worst of all it just stood there looking down at its knees. It was a pitiful sight and I suggested to my uncle that maybe the animal's fitness had expired. He was indignant and heatedly explained that what I saw in front of me was in fact an experienced donkey. In his opinion this was just the type of animal I needed to teach me the skill of negotiating the busy city streets. He assured me that after a few days, when it got over the disappointment of having to leave Golden Grove, the donkey would be fine.

I plodded slowly into the world of commerce a few weeks later, as the inexperienced driver of a small cart pulled by an experienced

The Golden Grove Express

donkey. My heart was full of the pride of ownership and a sense of control over my own destiny. A young man could wish for nothing more.

At first, I was ridiculed by the other cart men, as they referred to my donkey as "carrion crow bait". I had proudly painted the name "Golden Grove Express" on the side of my cart, but they quickly re-christened it the "Carrion Crow Compress". The problem of this eye-pass soon solved itself, as after a few months of Campbellville care, my donkey forgot about Golden Grove. It put on some weight, got a new rhythm to its step and was able to hold its head up high once more.

Eventually, I realised that my income was being severely limited by my "compressed cart" and I needed to invest in a larger horse-drawn model. The problem was that I had grown so attached to my donkey, which had unselfishly shared its experience of the streets with me, that I couldn't bring myself to get rid of him. As a compromise, I bought another donkey to work in tandem pulling a longer cart. This one was a large black donkey and my father said it was a Kentucky donkey from Leguan Island in the Essequibo River, whatever that meant.

There is a general rule that cart men and school children don't mix. Children often spend their bus fare then try to jump on to the passing cart for a free ride, to and from school. They were a nuisance to cart men, most of whom had a special long whip designed to clear the cart of schoolchildren. Because I was still a child of school age myself, I was an exception to this rule and welcomed them on my cart. At first they were surprised and suspicious when I invited them to take a ride but eventually we became trusted friends.

One day, shortly after I had bought my new cart, I was transporting a half-load of school children up Lamaha Street sharing some of their green mango, pepper and salt between us. A small boy who was sitting next to me observing the behaviour of my two donkeys remarked, "Mister, dem two donkeys you got dey just like Burnham and Jagan, one black and one grey and dey always fighting one anodda."

Children are often blessed with a certain clearness of thought that is seldom found in adults. With just a simple sentence this schoolboy had analysed the behaviour of my donkeys perfectly. From that day on I christened the donkeys, Forbes and Cheddie, and used these names whenever I had to discipline them.

My popularity grew with school children and my fellow cart men, as I became known as the man who had Forbes and Cheddie in harness. At the wharves and bonds where I made a living transporting cargo, workers and customers alike would ask me about my donkeys. It became a little game between us in which I would make up political reasons for any donkey disagreements that might occur, and was expected to provide a topical commentary about them. For example, "Why was Cheddie always biting Forbes when it was budget time in parliament?"

I even had to be careful how I used the whip in the presence of their respective supporters. As a result of this unique state of affairs, my business was booming and I was often given jobs in preference to other carts waiting in line that had nameless donkeys.

One day I was parked at the end of a long passageway in front of a bond, where I waited for my cart to be loaded. My donkeys seemed to be in a surprisingly agreeable mood so I took a chance to leave them unattended and go in search of the customer. Unfortunately, a noisy three-wheeled cart, with its engine mounted on the large front wheel, rumbled down the passageway and turned just behind where my cart was parked. Coughing and wheezing with some gas-oil congestion, it produced a particularly loud backfire. The Leguan donkey had never heard any sound resembling this during its peaceful life in its island home and using its best Essequibo instincts, bolted for safety.

With a savage jerk it tore the turntable off of the cart and, with it still in tow, the donkey careened down the passageway towards the freedom of busy Water Street. Dragging the piece of cart like a broken chariot, it scraped the walls of the passageway clean of all the workers' bicycles, something that the management of that particular company had been trying unsuccessfully to accomplish for years.

Hearing the shouts of, "De Jackass gone mad", I sprinted out of the bond and charged down the passageway in pursuit. But even though my time recorded over the distance was a personal best, I still couldn't catch Forbes. As he reached the gate I was close enough to see the expression of terror and disbelief on the faces of the two men riding a bicycle slowly across the path of the frantic animal. The rider slid off the back of the saddle and dived for cover, leaving his friend stranded on the bicycle with one leg over the handlebars. The bicycle slowed to a stop, "stickled" in the upright position for a few seconds then fell over on its side. The cyclist prayed for a miracle and watched with eyes bulging, as the crazed animal leapt towards him at full stride.

I stood, hands on head, waiting helplessly for the impact. Prayers were heard and answered. Just seconds before the collision, the shaft of the cart somehow hooked the gatepost and this arrested the donkey in mid-air. The exhausted animal stumbled and went down in a kneeling position almost on top of the man. Man and animal were now shoulder to shoulder, frozen with fright, regarding each other point blank, eyelashes touching. A dribble of froth from the donkey's nose fell on the cyclist's face and the spell was broken. Just as I snatched the donkey by the bridle and pulled him upright, the victim gave vent to a belated scream and scrambled to disentangle himself from bike and beast. I quickly tied the donkey and rushed over to the man and offered to pay for his flattened bicycle.

"De bike is one ting" shouted the victim, "but like you en see de donkey brace me. You know me heart stop beating? You lucky um start back."

The cyclist thought for a few seconds and then continued, "Plus de donkey dribble pun me face, all deese things does add up. We gun make one calculation together with the bike money."

He followed me back down the passageway towards my cart in silence, no doubt trying to decide on the price of a "brace and dribble" from a donkey.

My worries were far from over as the passageway was littered with damaged bicycles, which were being examined by their disgruntled owners. Just then, to my relief, I spotted a large sign that had been completely covered with bicycles before the incident, and was now in clear view. It read simply, "Lean no cycles, by order of the management". This gave my spirits a lift and I began to argue forcefully that, because of the sign, I was not responsible for any cycle repairs. There was a loud crash behind me and all arguments came to a halt. The strongest looking stevedore I had ever seen had thrown his damaged bicycle on to my empty cart and, towering over me, said in a soft, menacing voice, "I need it back for lunch-time". All I could do was nod my head feebly in agreement. This gesture was immediately interpreted by the other labourers as an admission of liability, and they all did likewise with their own bicycles. As I stood there looking at the cartload of bicycles, trying to figure out the total cost of their repairs, I remembered my father's warning about the necessity of a secondary education.

My gaze fell on my old, grey donkey that was still standing in its harness licking a fly from its nose. Through all the commotion Cheddie had never moved from his place in the cart. My uncle from Golden Grove was right, there is no substitute for "donkey experience", what a pity it is not available to humans.

The Rainbow

*W*hen God created the earth he found that in order to sustain life, it was necessary to supply the water needed by every living thing. This, of course, was a task of such great proportions that it could only be accomplished from the heavens above. A clever cycle was created with water falling from the clouds on the earth as rain, and then returning to the clouds as water vapour, to start the process all over again.

This system adequately quenched the earth for a time but a serious problem developed which was of grave concern to everyone living during that period. With each shower of rain the colours of the earth were washed away and things gradually began to fade. Eventually, everything was bleached to white or tones of light grey.

This was indeed a great catastrophe and both humans and animals became confused and disoriented. The whole world appeared as if it had been stained a whitish grey by the invisible ash of some giant volcano. Everything looked the same and people became depressed at the hopeless monotony of their existence.

It was hard to imagine the damage caused to the human spirit by this strange state of affairs. Days went by suddenly without the crimson, soothing balm of sunset to signal their ending. No more rose-colored tints in the eastern sky to herald the dawn. In fact, no one seemed to be really sure anymore which direction was east or west. This tragic transformation was most obvious in the sky. Clouds completely disappeared into the whiteness, so there were no more sunny or cloudy days. Each day was grey. As a result, people were never sure when rain would fall and were often caught far from shelter, without their umbrellas and raincoats. Even the horizon disappeared.

Animals were particularly affected. Without their spots or stripes to display, they appeared dejected. Those that ate grass and leaves lost their appetites, as they had trouble discerning their favourite diet from the tangled mass of grey before them. No one seemed to care about flowers anymore or even notice the dull butterflies and humming birds that flitted about them in confusion, trying to feed. The sense of smell took on a new importance as people became aware of the presence of blooms by the beauty of their scents.

Only the whistles of birds made people aware of their location and this particular skill brought new species to prominence. Macaws, parrots and toucans became just ugly, noisy birds that seemed clumsy in appearance. In contrast, the carrion crow was transformed into a silver eagle and now floated high above on its throne of wind, with newly appreciated elegance.

Camouflage among animals was no longer an art but just a part of the universal sameness that covered the land. Life seemed to be one long unending chore. The size, shape and texture of everything became crucial for identification. Everyone now saw things as if they were colour-blind and though they were familiar with the old adage that "colour was only skin deep", no one had ever taken this wisdom too literally. The importance of colour was now forcibly brought to their attention.

With everything stripped of the decoration and embellishment that so often cloud our judgment, the true worth of both people and things was immediately obvious. As the self-imposed dividing lines of colour could no longer be used, ethnic groups with their particular prejudices dissolved into the equality of one human race. This state of affairs had many benefits and brought people closer together. Young children even happily ate their "greens". However, after having experienced the earth in the full glory of all its tints and hues, this colourless state was unbearable.

The world suffered like this for a while, and as they always did when problems were totally beyond their control, everyone looked to the heavens for a solution. That is why "Heaven" came to be thought of as some place up above the sky where surely the ideal conditions must exist, since most solutions to earthly problems seemed to come from that direction. This particular problem was no exception.

One magic day, out of this same Heaven came the solution. Every shower of rain was now accompanied by a rainbow consisting of all the variations of colour needed to replenish the colours of the earth. In this new system, as the rain washed the colours away they were immediately replaced by transfusions from a rainbow. In this way a delicate balance could easily be maintained.

Even today, thousands of years later, some people still experience colour-blindness as a reminder to us all of the lessons that must be learnt concerning the abuse and prejudices associated with colour in our daily lives.

A Set of Lights

*F*or the third time I stumbled up what I prayed would be the last hill. From its summit I gazed with relief at the group of buildings that nestled like bird's eggs in the half open palm of the North Pakaraima Mountains.

My destination was known simply as "The Landing", because like so many similar porknocker settlements in the interior of Guyana, it was located on the bank of a river. I had hoped to make my own landing there three days before, but high up in the river, where it shakes itself loose from the mountain's grasp, I had almost drowned.

I had planned to take some time off from prospecting for gold and diamonds to make a new corial, but had repeatedly put it off. My old canoe seemed to sense just what I expected of it, with the minimum guidance from my paddle. It was like a faithful friend that had taken me safely through dangerous rapids where few had dared to venture. I just couldn't bring myself to discard such old and trusted companion.

The night before I began my journey the rain had wrapped the forest in a long, intimate embrace. In the morning, the river was not in a mood for small corials, and as I was swept along at its surging will, it seemed to bare its foaming fangs at every opportunity. Rounding a particularly sudden bend, I barely managed to out-manoeuvre a freshly uprooted Mora tree, but couldn't avoid the head of a rock waiting in ambush just below the surface. With that resounding crack that wood makes when it is being torn from itself, the corial split like a giant seed pod, scattering its contents to feed the hungry river.

I had saved nothing but my life and my "kiddy" of small diamonds that I always kept in an old, plastic Vicks inhaler case, firmly tied around my neck with a shoelace. Having run out of food I was hoping to use this modest accumulation of "fine breeze', as the shop keeper would surely refer to my diamonds, to purchase the ration needed for another month's work in the backdam.

After walking the last three days without food, I rolled down that final hill like a vehicle travelling on its rims, its tires long having been used up. I strained every sense to try to detect the prevailing mood of the landing before actually reaching it, as this would be crucial to the success of my mission and maybe even my very survival.

The smoke from the logie drifted towards me on a "sometime-ish" land breeze and brought with it the distinct smell of Marmite stew. This was a good sign as Marmite usually meant wild meat. This smell was seasoned with the sound of calypso music and the familiar refrain of "Good morning Mr Walker, I come to see your daughter", was barely discernible in the distance. After walking for so many days, the chorus of this song took on a more personal meaning. The music of the Mighty Sparrow was always a sign of prosperity on any landing and was preferable to the hard luck songs of Jim Reeves, which were also interior jukebox favourites when things were hard. I tried not to be overcome by optimism, but all the signs were good.

I ducked under the barbed wire clothesline, with its usual assortment of thin, tired, porknocker garments, and reached the logie where a stew pot was boiling unattended. Loud voices that were competing with the jukebox could be heard from the shop next door. At ten in the morning this could only mean one thing, liquor was flowing. Somebody had struck it very rich and was "stamping" the landing, partying night and day until either money ran out or the plane from Georgetown arrived. Whichever happened first was all the same to the porknocker.

I brushed aside the small pig, with chiggers between its toes and a peel-necked fowl cock that were fighting over a dead lizard, and entered the shop. To my surprise, only three porknockers and Chinee, the shopkeeper, were present. It was a typical "landing shop", where the smell of fresh fireside smoke and stale fish blended with the sweet odour of liquor fumes, evaporating from the mouths of men and open bottles.

"Wha happenin Small Boy, yuh land. Come tek a drink, yuh lookin lil wash out," said the oldest of the porknockers. He was a frail, Portuguese man called Gunboat, who had a pink face where wrinkles and varicose veins seemed to continuously jostle one another for a better position.

"Eh! Smallee, like water more than corn flour boy. Like yuh could barely fetch yuh perspiration. Wha wrong"? asked Matt Cobern, tilting his grey cowboy hat to one side. No one had ever seen Matt without his hat. Whether sleeping in his hammock or bathing by the waterside his hat was always in place. Chinee, who had known him since he was a young boy, had never seen his head but said that his hat had been white when it was new.

To this half-sober gathering of bush veterans I attempted to report on my limited success in prospecting a new area near the source of the Potaro River, but was rudely interrupted by Angle Iron. He was a massive man from St Lucia, with skin like alligator back and muscles bulging everywhere, even on his face.

"Prospecting! al yuh now-a-days porknockers don't know bout dat. Al yuh does prospect wid yuh ears, listening for odder people shout", he growled.

It was Angle Iron who was buying the drinks and I imagined the reason he got his name was because from whatever angle you viewed him, he looked like a large piece of well-sculpted iron.

On the table were four empty bottles and a fifth already below the label. They were drinking Tatuzinho, that old Brazilian favourite. "Tatu" is the Brazilian word for armadillo and this animal was proudly displayed on the label of each bottle. "Zinho" probably meant high spirits, as only an armadillo was immune to the high spirits caused by the drinking of this brew. I knew that if I took a drink on my "three-day" empty stomach that I would be like a monkey in a molasses barrel. To avoid this I stepped to the counter and called for two packets of Break-o-day salt biscuits.

Although I was thirty years old and had spent the last twelve years of my life porknocking for gold and diamonds in the bush bottom, to men like these I would always be an inexperienced small boy. In answer to their questions I began to relate the story of my lucky escape from the raging river. I didn't get very far before Gunboat interrupted, "Young people stupit, you see da rain wuh pass de odder night an you still gone in de river. When you see rain like da you mus use wha God give yuh, yuh brains an yuh two foot. God en give yuh boat an paddle".

"Da was a bad rain in truth," added Matt Coburn, "even dem crapo did looking fa shelter. But yuh can't say dat boy stupit because he bin Queens College in Georgetown. You ever bin anyway Gunboat?"

The old man's face got even pinker at this personal attack on his intelligence and he declared, "I bin Walker's Under 12 in Kitty. In me days dem teacha did so good dat me larn all me need fuh know fuh town life, since me was twelve years old. Now bush life is a nodda ting. Yuh got fa larn dat till yuh dead and if Small Boy don't larn um fass, he go dead early".

Angle Iron, who was the most drunk of the lot, was looking for a place to lie down. He climbed onto a bag of saltfish and said in a "Tatuzinho" voice, "Smallee stupit yes, he believe dat yuh does only see 'raindeer' in rainy season". Before I could say anything in my defence, his snores fell into to the same rhythm as the duke box.

"Well from them fine diamond Small Boy does bring fuh sell me, he mus no bout needle fuh record player, dat is all dey good fuh," Chinee chuckled. No part of the shopkeeper resembled a Chinese, but he was quite proud of the fact that he had grown up in a Hong Kong Chinese cookshop in Lombard Street and could speak Chinese fluently.

"Leh we tess Smallee brains," the shopkeeper continued. De adda night all awee sid down by de cashew tree and we see a brite light speed across de sky like Accouri wen dag chase am. Me and Matt Coburn say it was a satellite, but da jackass Gunboat say it was de Skylab. Wa you say it is Small Boy?"

This question was of course impossible for me to answer since I had not seen the object about which they were arguing. However, I realised that this was not only a chance for me to earn the respect of these seasoned porknockers, but that my entire reputation on the landing was at stake. I had to find an answer that would impress them.

Thankfully, before I could say anything, Gunboat got up from the table for emphasis and put on his best English. "Listen Small Boy, you don't knows nutting bout sky and stars, dat is bush larnin. All awee who see um agree dat de ting only had one light, so it gat to be de Skylab. You en hear wa de white people name um, if um had more dan one light, it woulda be a set-a-lights".

The Old Dog

The Old Dog dozing in the sun was awakened by a strong feline scent. He raised his head and through bloodshot eyes he saw a young cat, tail held high, passing by not six feet from where he lay. I must really be in bad shape to warrant such disrespect, he thought. Not too long ago he would have chased her tail all over the neighbourhood, but now he just flopped back down on the concrete and dozed off. Sleeping in the sun was the only thing that seemed to ease the pain in his joints these days and in his fitful dreams he usually reviewed his long, exciting dog's life.

His had been a good life compared to what some other dogs had to go through. He especially felt sorry for those who were kept as "slaves", or "pets", as humans referred to them. These poor dogs were collared and chained and forced to work for their masters. Some were taught to do tricks, which was just another name for work. They were trained to hunt, fetch newspapers, and perform tricks for the entertainment of their master's friends. Others were put on guard duty and were expected to risk their lives to protect their owners and their property. As an added torment they were frequently bathed in an attempt to destroy their natural scent that is so important in a dog's life. But by far the worst act of degradation they suffered was being told if, when, and with whom they must mate. This was contrary to the most important fundamental law of a dog's life. It was true that these "slaves" were fed regularly, but this could not compensate for the underprivileged life they had to endure.

The Old Dog had never suffered these indignities, as he had always been free and ownerless, the way it was meant to be. Humans, of course, were strongly opposed to this freedom and not only branded him a 'stray', but felt that an owner must be found for him. He had successfully eluded them in his youth and at this stage of his life he was safe, as no one wanted to own an old dog that didn't have long to

The Old Dog

live. The more he thought of it the more he realised that humans were the cause of most of the problems in a dog's life. They seemed to be obsessed with dogs and to make matters worse they kept inventing stupid sayings about their relationship with them that were completely false.

One of their favourites of mistaken wisdom was, "The dog is man's best friend". Did dogs have a choice? Shouldn't everyone be able to choose his friends? With so many other dogs to choose from, why would they choose humans? This would be the same as if dogs were to say, "Fleas are the dog's best friend". No dog would be stupid enough to believe that. A flea's best friend is obviously another flea. Fleas only tolerate dogs like dogs tolerate humans, as providers of food and shelter, not as friends. As far as dogs are concerned fleas and humans are just another itching part of life.

Another saying which always annoyed the Old Dog whenever he heard it was, "Every dog has its day". Why should a dog only have a single day? This definitely did not apply to him as he had spent many years as "Top Dog" of several neighbourhoods. He usually had more female admirers than he could lick, and the only reason he would change neighbourhoods was because of a dwindling food supply. Every dog knows that too many female companions and not enough food is a recipe for physical disaster. As these happy times filled the Old Dog's dreams his back leg twitched and he gave that gentle, pleasant sigh that only sleeping dogs make.

Humans were even disrespectful of old dogs, he thought. They believed that you couldn't train an old dog to do new tricks due to some hard-headedness on the old dog's part. Little did they know that all dogs hated to be taught new tricks, but it was only the older dogs that had the courage to bluntly refuse to be trained. Humans should be careful because training sometimes backfired, resulting in the trainer becoming the trained. He had witnessed many instances where dogs had skilfully trained their masters to perform. Some only had to scratch the door whenever they wanted to be taken for a walk. Other lazier dogs trained their masters to take them for drives in their cars at special times every evening. Believe it or not, he had heard fantastic stories of places far away where dogs had actually trained their masters to follow them, with a spoon and a plastic bag, cleaning up their mess as fast as they could make it. These stories seemed too far-fetched and the Old Dog could not bring himself to believe that humans could be that stupid.

Suddenly he was awakened by the incessant buzzing of a large fly that was trying to land on the sore he had on his left ear. From it's irregular buzz he could tell it was the same fly that had bothered him yesterday. Not long ago he used to bite flies in mid-air, but recently his reflexes had almost slowed to a halt. He thought of using his open mouth as a trap, but he doubted whether he could close it fast enough to catch the fly.

The Old Dog got up, stretched, and with an aging stiff-legged walk, moved out of the shadow of the cake-shop and lay down again in the sun on the warm pavement at the side of the road. He was careful not to go too near the edge as nowadays vehicles would swerve from potholes and run up on the pavement. Ever since he was a young dog he had been terrified of being killed by a car like so many of his friends. He often wondered how he would die. He felt that the morning might soon come when his eyes just wouldn't open. In fact even now he was having trouble opening his right eye every morning and the Old Dog wondered if this meant that he was already half dead.

The Bird Watcher

As soon as Beckwith Titmus settled himself in the seat of the BWIA Sunjet, he knew that his bird watching trip to South America would be a great success. How could he fail when the upholstery of the cabin of the aircraft was decorated with scarlet ibises in various postures of flight? Beckwith had chosen Guyana for his trip because it was the only English-speaking nation on the continent and he felt that both the language and culture of the former British colony would be similar to that of his homeland.

Beckwith had been unable to find any illustrated books on the birds of Guyana. Instead, he had purchased *The Birds of Suriname* to use as a reference to identify the many species he hoped to see during his trip. He spent the long hours of the flight pouring over the pictures of the Suriname birds and hoped that, like himself, they would all be making the trip to Guyana shortly.

After an uneventful flight, the aircraft landed safely and had nearly come to a stop in front of the terminal building, when pandemonium broke out. The Guyanese passengers all jumped up from their seats as if in answer to some silent alarm. Beckwith thought he was experiencing an emergency evacuation of the aircraft as the passengers jostled and elbowed him in a mad dash for the exit. When he at last got his chance to disembark, he stopped dead halfway down the steps of the aircraft. He couldn't believe his good fortune. Sitting on a flagpole not fifty yards away was a species of falcon that he had never seen before. Beckwith fumbled excitedly in his haversack for his binoculars to make a proper identification of this raptor. The fat lady behind him, who was juggling four overstuffed pieces of hand baggage, ploughed into him.

Beckwith Titmus and three pieces of baggage tumbled loudly down the aluminium staircase and came to rest on the tarmac in an undignified heap. He felt as though he was trapped on a runaway baggage carousel and as he disentangled himself the fat woman, worried about her fragile hand baggage, gave Beckwith his first Guyanese opinion on the intelligence of foreigners. "Wait is stupit white people stupit, you en know dat steps make fuh walk pun, not fuh stan up", she bellowed, "Yuh better hope nun of me tings en bruk, because if yuh could only afford one hand piece, yuh en gun able pay fuh me Englun tings".

Beckwith did not understand this strange dialect and he smiled at the lady thinking that she was apologising for causing him discomfort. The fat lady just snatched up her things, sucked her teeth in disgust, and stormed off towards the terminal mumbling, "White people don't understan simple tings". Of course by now the falcon had long fled the flagpole.

Beckwith shared a minibus to Georgetown with other passengers. Fortunately, he had decided to keep his haversack with him, as this prevented strangers from sitting on his lap when the bus became overcrowded. It was an exciting journey during which he experienced many unfamiliar phenomena. For instance, he saw three men pushing a large bus and couldn't help wondering how far they were going. As the minibus hurtled through some areas, herds of various semi-domesticated animals took over the roadway. Without reducing speed the bus driver skilfully wove between this live obstacle course, sometimes using the grassy parapets, dangerously close to the canals at the edge of the cane fields. But it was the bird life that amazed him most. Beckwith thought he saw at least twenty different species of birds during the trip, but couldn't be sure. From the speeding bus even the traffic policemen were just a blur.

Beckwith awakened in the 'Nest' next morning to the cheerful sound of birdsong. He had chosen that particular guesthouse because of its name, and although it was situated in the heart of the city, it sounded as though he was in the middle of a bird sanctuary. The ripening fruit of the mango tree near his bedroom window was like a magnet to many fruit-eating species and Beckwith was entertained by an intricate blend of calls and whistles. He had no trouble identifying them all and as the guesthouse gardener supplied him with the local names, he realised how important it would be to hire a guide for his trip to the interior.

Beckwith was advised that the best place to contact a guide would be at the Amerindian Hostel in Princess Street. In his search for the hostel he approached two rough looking men he saw standing at the corner of the road to ask directions. They showed him a knife and asked him for all the money he had. Beckwith didn't quite understand what they were saying and thought that they wanted to sell him the knife.

"I am afraid that I don't have any funds that I can spare right now," Beckwith apologised.

"You like you want somebody bore you", replied the man with the knife as he moved toward Beckwith menacingly. But before the exchange of funds could be concluded, a passer-by in a car intervened, the robbers dispersed and Beckwith was taken to the hostel. He managed to procure the services of Ciprian Peters from Malali village in the upper Demerara River, who was familiar with the particular area where Beckwith wanted to go.

During the long drive on the white sand trail through the dense rainforest Beckwith was bubbling with excitement at how many forest species he was able to identify and add to his handwritten catalogue. He continuously regaled his stoical Amerindian guide with the scientific names of the birds they saw and the habits peculiar to each species. Beckwith was disappointed that this vast reservoir of knowledge failed to impress his companion. Ciprian, who had never observed a species like Beckwith at close range before, was by this time totally fed up with his incessant bird chatter and devised a plan to gain some relief.

A few minutes before three in the afternoon he suddenly instructed Beckwith to stop the vehicle in the middle of the trail where there were tall trees on either side. The guide explained to the Englishman that this was in fact one of the many toucan crossings located throughout the rainforest, where every day at precisely three o'clock, toucans would fly across the roadway. Beckwith glanced at his watch and burst out laughing, it was two minutes to three. He was about to speak when, not a hundred yards ahead, the most beautiful Toco Toucan he had ever seen glided slowly across the trail, from one large tree to another. Beckwith was flabbergasted. Before he could ask any of the many questions that raced through his mind, Ciprian casually remarked, "The toucan is a bit early today and we almost missed its crossing."

Beckwith drove on in silence for the rest of the day, questioning both his eyesight and the logic of what he had witnessed. He had been talking so much that he failed to notice the first of the pair of toucans when it flew across the trail. The Amerindian knew from experience that its mate would soon follow and with a quick glance at Beckwith's watch, he decided to play a trick on the birdwatcher. After this incident the Englishman overcame the urge to educate the Amerindian and became his student instead. He learnt that Amerindians don't talk to the forest and its creatures, they listen to them. For the rest of the trip, without his companion's annoying chatter, Ciprian basked in the soothing sounds of the forest that always seemed to recharge his soul.

With more than four hundred species already recorded since his arrival, Beckwith was advised to investigate the rich bird life of the Essequibo coast. He noticed from his map that this area boasted of villages with good English names such as Dartmouth, Queenstown and Adventure and he eagerly made arrangements to visit the region. He took a ferry across the Demerara River and reluctantly boarded a train of such vintage, he was sure that its birth certificate could not be found. Although consisting of only four carriages, the antique engine was so busy converting firewood into black smoke that it only just managed to drag its load across the coastal lowlands towards its final destination of Parika on the Essequibo River. The stealth of the train suited Beckwith's purpose as it crept up to the birds without scaring them and he managed to identify many new species from the rice fields that surrounded the train line.

After his initial excitement subsided, Beckwith became aware of a young East Indian boy and girl that shared the train compartment with him. They offered him some of their plantain chips and struck up a conversation. Beckwith Titmus introduced himself to his new friends but was disappointed at their laughter on hearing his name. They claimed it was the funniest name they had ever heard and asked him if there were more like him where he came from. On enquiring he discovered that the brother and sister were Rohit and Chandrawattie Ramcharitar, but they invited him to call them Ro and Chandra. Beckwith managed to control his amusement at the strange sound of their names and for the first time in his life, he suggested that he be referred to as Beck. It didn't take long for Beck's trained, birdwatcher's eye to identify Chandra's smouldering, eastern beauty, and as she got off the train at Stewartville, she pointed out the house where she lived and invited him to stop in on his return journey from the Essequibo.

The Essequibo Coast lived up to its reputation as over the next week Beck added more than a hundred new birds to his list. However, romantic images of Chandra continuously glided across his mind like some erotic species of graceful egret he couldn't quite identify. With excited anticipation Beckwith Titmus boarded the train at Parika, but to his dismay he discovered that it travelled even more slowly against the wind. He disembarked at Stewartville and hurried towards Chandra's house. He saw her from a distance but she seemed to be acting rather strangely. Chandra was stooping down by the side of the canal in front of her house, viciously beating a piece of cloth with a heavy wooden paddle. The Englishman wondered if she had done something wrong and was being punished by her parents for it.

Rohit came from the rice field at the back of the house and greeted Beck like a long-lost friend. He went into the yard with Chandra by his side and was introduced to her parents. Liliwattie Ramcharitar, a surprisingly young woman who looked as though she could have been her daughter's twin, smiled and offered Beck a limp, calloused hand in the form of a greeting. Hardatt her husband, who was weeding in the yard, came towards them cutlass still in hand. With his measuring smile he looked like an alligator with gold teeth that even flashed in the shade. After the introductions were completed, they all sat on the front steps of the house until dark, with Beck trying his best to explain the vast differences of his life in England as compared to theirs in Guyana.

Dinner was an education for the Englishman as it consisted of some part of the sheep's entrails, that he was certain was still new to science, and curry duck. Beckwith stared at the head of the unknown species of duck floating in profile in the curry sauce and lost his appetite for both food and bird watching at the same time.

Beck was disappointed that at no time during the evening did he get a chance to speak to Chandra alone. Her father always seemed to be strategically placed between them to prevent any communication. When he awoke the next morning he was overjoyed to find that during the night a small piece of paper had been placed in his close fist. It was a note from Chandra which said, "I will come to meet you in Georgetown. Where are you staying?" Beck quickly scribbled his reply on a piece of paper but realised that he would have to be extremely careful how he slipped it to Chandra. Hardatt had resumed the close watch of the evening before and the whole family accompanied him to the station when he went to catch the train for Georgetown. Beck had the crumpled note in the palm of his hand and as he shook hands with Chandra in the full glare of Hardatt's suspicious gaze, the message reached its destination. On the train Beckwith Titmus forgot about the birds he had come to see and whistled tunelessly to himself. He lost himself in planning how he would spend a glorious week at the Nest in Georgetown with Chandrawattie Ramcharitar.

Early next morning, before the birds could assemble at their 'mango restaurant' outside his window, Beckwith was awakened by a soft rap on his bedroom door. He opened it to find Chandrawattie standing there with a shy, grown-up smile on her face and an overnight bag in her hand. With her hair and skin freshly anointed with coconut oil she glistened in the morning light and to Beck she was like some highly scented exotic flower. Chandra was overwhelmed by the luxury and high cost of his room at the Nest and convinced him to move to her aunt's house in Kitty, where they could stay for free. Beck, like most Englishmen, had always found freeness to be a useful thing, and not realising the danger he readily agreed to the move.

The following morning while Beck and Chandra lay wrapped like curry and roti in blissful sleep, they were awakened by a commotion. Chandra's relatives seemed to be having a loud argument with someone in front of the yard. Beckwith, who had never heard anything like this before, rushed to the window to investigate. Standing on the bridge he was surprised to see Chandra's father, cutlass in hand as usual, arguing at the top of his voice with Chandra's aunt. When he saw Beckwith at the window Hardatt flew into an uncontrollable rage and began to scream incoherently at him. His newly-sharpened cutlass flashed coded messages of violence in the early morning sun.

Beckwith did not understand most of what the enraged man was saying, but he was able to decipher that Hardatt was inviting him downstairs to have some sort of discussion. Just as he was about to go, Chandra ran out of the bedroom crying and held on to his leg with both hands to prevent him from moving. "Don't go," she begged, "he gun kill you."

"Surely not," Beck replied. He had seen no gun in Hardatt's possession and had no idea what the man's ranting was all about.

"Come down hey you chile tief, I gun chap up you ass," screamed Hardatt. Beck pleaded with Chandra to let go of his leg so that he could go and reason with her father and get this matter settled, however she only wailed louder, "You don't understan, he gun kill you".

Hardatt's voice could be heard clearly through the window, "Bring you white backside dung stays, I gun chap you up in pound parcels".

By now Beckwith was beginning to get the gist of Hardatt's diatribe, but he couldn't understand the reason for it. Chandrawattie had not told him that she had left her Stewartville home in the early morning without telling her family, and that her overnight bag not only contained all the good clothes she possessed but her passport as well. In fact, her father was right to believe that Beckwith was about to kidnap his daughter and take her back to England with him. Not aware of these facts Beck felt that the only way to end this embarrassing situation was to go downstairs and discuss the matter like two gentlemen, but Chandra would not let go of his leg.

"Let me go downstairs and chat with your father," he begged her again.

Chandra only became more agitated. "You don't understand English, he gun chap you up in pound parcels wid he cutlish," she cried.

The Englishman's feelings were hurt. Never before in his life had he ever been accused of not understanding the English language. He thought for a while in silence and suddenly the gravity of the matter at hand finally dawned on his British-thinking mind. "Chandra," he said, with a slight tremor of fear in his voice, "I weigh one hundred and fifty two pounds. Are you trying to tell me that your father, for some reason known only to himself, is seriously considering carving me into one hundred and fifty two separate parcels?"

"Yes," Chandra said softly and let go of Beckwith's leg.

Armed and Dangerous

*A*s usual, Amelia Bancroft was surprised to wake up in the morning and get a chance to greet another new day. She was eighty-seven on her last birthday and although she felt fairly strong, she really didn't know how a person of her age was supposed to feel. Over the past year she had been experiencing a pain in her chest whenever she exerted herself too much. Her old "dispenser friend" at the drugstore had told her that she may get heart trouble later on in life, but it was nothing to worry about.

Ever since this diagnosis she had felt that the morning might soon come when she would just not wake up. She had no fear of death but was curious about how her life would eventually come to an end. Like all good books the ending was important and she didn't want to miss it. She had lived in Kitty all her life. First in her parent's house in Pike Street and after she got married she had moved to a small cottage in Gordon Street where she still lived.

Sixty-nine years ago she had met and married Turner Bancroft, a Barbadian gentleman who was twelve years older than her. As the daughter of a pastor, Amelia had led a sheltered life and was therefore completely swept away by Turner's Caribbean charm. As a teenager she was easily impressed and even found his abrasive "Bajan" accent romantic. Turner had portrayed himself as the son of a well-to-do Barbadian family who had come to British Guiana to seek his fortune in the Potaro gold fields. Unfortunately, his fortune had turned out to be more elusive than he had expected and Turner had turned out to be just another foreign con man.

When she was younger Amelia had worked as a domestic to help make ends meet. Her husband did not have a fixed income and times were extremely hard. God in all his wisdom had blessed her with no children and it was only now, in the loneliness of her old age, that she began to question this wisdom. Her husband with his usual thoughtlessness had gone and died suddenly many years ago. To Amelia's surprise, Turner had actually owned the small cottage where they lived in Gordon Street and it was the only thing he had left in his will for her. It seems that some of his clever schemes must have been successful after all.

Amelia had worked until old age had overtaken her. Now she was forced to exist on a meagre Government Old Age Pension and the produce from a small kitchen garden at the back of her yard. Every time she drew her pension at the Kitty post office she would remark, "If dey could only afford to give me dis pittance de Government must be brokes. Somebody should give dem a raise."

Amelia was known by everyone in her neighbourhood as Ma Bancroft or just Ma to little children. Her life had become a predictably boring affair. The high point of each week was a trip to the supermarket where she couldn't buy what she needed but only what she could afford. This was ironic because in the olden days when she used to work for money there were countrywide shortages of foodstuff and as a result, she couldn't get what she needed then either.

It was Thursday again, the day Ma Bancroft chose to do her shopping every week so as to avoid the crowds. Most people didn't realise that shopping for food was serious business; you had to take your time. In her case it was mostly like window-shopping from inside the store. She got a chance to carefully examine all the items in the supermarket especially the new products. She enjoyed this immensely and fantasised about which ones she would buy if she could afford it. She knew all the supermarket employees and they allowed her to stay as long as she wanted before checking out with the same three or four inexpensive items every week.

Ma's favourite place in the whole supermarket was the shelf with the chocolates. She loved the heavenly aroma that hung in the air around this shelf. She would inhale deeply and it was like a tonic to her aging lungs. She was always amazed to see all the different varieties of chocolates. They came in all shapes and sizes, bars, balls and boxes, with nuts, raisins, cereal and biscuits inside of them. The only one she couldn't figure out was white chocolate, wasn't that some sort of contradiction. What she liked best were those large heart-shaped gift boxes of chocolates with their red ribbon bows. Where were these things long ago when she had money to spend?

Ma wondered if Turner Bancroft was alive, if he would have bought one of these beautiful boxes of chocolates for her birthday. She doubted it, because he had once told her that they don't usually celebrate birthdays in Barbados.

Ma Bancroft ended her chocolate dreams and moved towards the cashier with the same four items that she had bought last week in her basket. A pint of brown rice, a small piece of local saltfish, two packets of salt biscuits and a cake of salt soap. She was lucky that she was still able to plant her kitchen garden next to the alley behind her house. It sometimes provided her with squash, pumpkin and tomatoes and all the pak choy, bora and fresh seasoning she needed to keep her pot boiling. This morning when she was passing in Pike Street on the way to the supermarket her good friend had called out to her and gave her two Buxton spice mangoes in a black plastic bag. She had lodged the bag of mangoes in the bag bay at the supermarket. She now collected it from the decent young fellow that worked there and left for home. The old lady walked slowly down the road smiling. She couldn't wait to get home and eat one the mangoes, she felt that it was going to be a good week for her.

Ma Bancroft put the bag on the table and hurried into the kitchen to get one of her enamel plates and the sharp kitchen knife to peel a mango. She emptied the contents of the black plastic bag on the top of her rickety dining table and to her amazement instead of mangoes a gun bounced once on the tabletop, skidded off and landed on the floor. Ma was in a state of severe shock. She stood perfectly still at first with her gaze firmly fixed on the gun which was lying just a few feet away from her. After what to her felt like a long time but was in fact only a few seconds, the old lady began to tremble uncontrollably. Then the pain in her chest started. She stumbled to her bedroom and threw herself across the bed. She experienced a new sensation, as if bats were fluttering in her chest as she gradually fell into a deep, exhausted sleep.

When Ma Bancroft awakened she naturally thought that it had been all a bad dream. Her palpitations had subsided and she felt perfectly normal again. She realised that it was after five o'clock as the sun had already dipped behind the coconut tree at the side of the house. This surprised her, as she usually never slept for long in the daytime. The old lady was hungry and as she made her way to the kitchen, her dream came true. The gun was lying on the floor just where she had left it.

Ma reversed slowly until she reached the rocking chair and sat down. Her eyes never left the weapon. She treated it as though it was a poisonous snake coiled and ready to strike.

In all of her eighty-seven years she had never seen anything like this. Like some miracle of Satan two mangoes had been transformed into a gun. She racked her rusty brain for a reasonable explanation but came up with a throbbing headache instead. Ma Bancroft remembered clearly seeing the two mangoes when her friend gave her the bag but there was no sign of them now. After many mind-searching hours, in between thoughts, it came suddenly to the confused old lady. The boy at the bag bay of the supermarket had given her the wrong bag by mistake. She would just have to take it back and exchange it like the time she had found ants on the salt fish.

However, this was not salt fish, this was a firearm and that was a lot different. From the moment she had brought the parcel home she had become an unlicensed firearm holder. She had often seen photographs of that kind of people in the newspapers on their way from court to jail. Ma didn't know what to do but realised that she would have to hide the gun carefully in case friends dropped in. She was scared to hold it so she got the pointa broom and tried to sweep it into the broom- cupboard. The gun wouldn't move, it just kept spinning around on the floor. Every time the muzzle pointed at Ma she would jump back and then walk around the back of it as though it were a living thing, and try to sweep it again. She eventually had to get the mortar stick and push it into the cupboard.

Ma Bancroft hardly slept that night. She was wide awake when the peel-necked fowl cock flew on to the neighbour's paling to welcome the dawn with its first crow. She wanted to return the gun to its rightful owner if only she knew who he was. It certainly did not belong to the boy in the bag bay at the supermarket and she was sure he would deny giving it to her. If her husband, Turner, was alive he would have probably sold it to the highest bidder; however, she was well past the age for gun running. When she got out of bed, for the first time in years, Ma noticed that there was a certain excitement in the air. She had an important secret that nobody else in the whole world knew. She was the owner of a firearm.

Although she was scared, Ma went to the broom cupboard as quietly as she could and peeped in. Thank goodness the gun lay on its side near the dustpan, facing the back of the cupboard. It didn't look as dangerous as it did yesterday, she thought. She wondered if it was loaded. As Ma Bancroft went about her daily chores the gun was all she could think about. While weeding in her kitchen garden she remembered the incident a short while ago when she had caught a man stealing her prized pumpkin that she had nurtured for many weeks. She had begged him not to take it but he just laughed at her. To make matters worse as he jumped over the paling he said to her, "Ah coming back fuh de squash soon, must care it good fuh me, hear old girl." Ma had felt so helpless that she just sat down in the middle of the pumpkin vine and started to cry. She now checked on the squash and was surprised it was still there.

"Leh he come now, ah would shoot he backside wid me gun," Ma said out loud, surprising herself. She looked around to make sure no one had heard her. She would have to be more careful. She went back into the house smiling to herself and took another peep at the gun in the cupboard. The old lady felt a lot safer with it close by.

As the weeks went by Ma Bancroft made her weekly visits to the supermarket and nobody asked her about the mistaken bag with the gun or the mangoes that were left unclaimed. She felt the euphoria of someone who had committed a crime and had skilfully escaped without a trace. For the first time in her life she somehow felt smart. As a result of her Christian upbringing, somewhere deep inside Ma felt a twinge of conscience but she had no intention of letting this ruin the newfound excitement in her life.

The old lady decided it was time she found out if the gun was loaded. Suppose the day came when she suddenly had to use it to protect herself. She would look really stupid if she tried to shoot someone without bullets. Ma had never held a gun before and she was scared. Her husband Turner liked Western films and would often take her to the Hollywood Cinema to see cowboy pictures. Over and over she had seen the cowboys load their guns by inserting bullets into the openings in the round parts and spinning them. She would have to examine the gun carefully.

It took a few weeks for her to summon up the courage but eventually Ma realised that it couldn't be avoided any longer, she had to handle the gun. She opened the cupboard and with her heart racing, she picked up the gun from the floor where it had lain for almost a month. She was surprised at how heavy it was. It must be full of bullets, she thought as she put it on the table. Sure enough on closer inspection, she could clearly see the backs of two bullets in the chambers of the gun. Ma sat at the table and played with her new toy awhile. Holding it in both her trembling hands she practiced aiming it at the kitchen stove. Although this was the biggest object in the house, she could only keep the gun pointed towards it for a few seconds before it started to shake and she was forced to put it back on the table.

Despite her age, every time Ma Bancroft handled the gun it gave her an intoxicating sense of power. She now had the means to defend herself from all danger. No one could take advantage of her any longer. She felt a new independence. She went to the window overlooking the kitchen garden in the back yard and braced the gun on the windowsill the way she had seen the cowboys do it in the movies. It hardly shook. She did the same with the window overlooking the front gate and felt satisfied that she had the whole yard covered. Ma was not afraid of the gun anymore and kept it in the drawer of her beside table under some old newspapers.

It became part of her daily routine that as soon as she awoke in the morning she would imagine that she had heard some one at the front gate. She would scramble her gun and shuffle to the window as fast as she could, and assume a shooting position. In mid-morning she would do the same for the back window. After a few weeks of these security drills Ma found she was getting quicker at it and the pain in her left hip had disappeared. For the first time in many years the old lady felt alive as opposed to simply waiting to die.

Ma Bancroft then became stricken by the same urge that all firearm holders sooner or later suffer from, the urge to shoot something or somebody. The old lady wanted to see if the gun really worked; if it could, in fact, do what it was manufactured to do, kill. She silently prayed for an attack on her house or kitchen garden. At least once before she died she wanted to go into action.

Although Ma's eyesight was good for a woman of her age, she was increasingly having problems hearing properly. Most times, when strangers spoke to her she would just smile as she was ashamed to ask them to repeat themselves. When walking on the road she was always careful to look behind her as she no longer heard the scooters and minibuses speeding through the narrow roads of Kitty. She had a small radio that was her constant companion around the house and this kept her up to date with the news. Ma now had to go closer and closer to the radio in order to hear it and she prayed that she would die before she stopped hearing it all together.

The only other problem Ma had was with the Guyana Power & Light Company. She had two small florescent lights in her house and as result used very little electricity. Although she always paid her bills on time at the Kitty post office, G.P.L. kept sending meter readers to check to see if her meter was working. Eventually, she got a letter from them accusing her of stealing current and inviting her to visit their head office in Main Street to discuss a settlement. Ma was very annoyed and as going to town by herself was stressful for her, she had ignored the notice completely.

One morning, in the middle of her security drill, Ma Bancroft was sitting on a stool at the back window. As usual she had the gun on the windowsill aiming at imaginary intruders in her kitchen garden. The G.P.L. disconnection crew came to the front of the house and rattled the gate. Getting no response the foreman of the group went up the front steps and rapped on the side of the small cottage. After once again receiving no answer he continued up the steps to the front door which was open, and stepped inside the house.

Up to this point Ma had heard nothing. However, the vibration of a loose floorboard alerted her to the presence of someone in her house. In very slow motion she swivelled round from the window with her gun held firmly in both hands to face the intruder. At the same instant the stool overbalanced and Ma Bancroft pulled the trigger with all her might. She heard the exciting roar of the gun as both she and the stool tumbled backwards into a corner. The bullet caused another hole in her already "holy" zinc roof. The G.P.L. foreman disconnected himself from the cottage with the speed of light. Ma got up as if in a trance and, as she had practiced so many times before, hurried towards the front window, gun in hand.

The fugitive stood on the old lady's bridge surrounded by his colleagues who were unsuccessfully trying to find out what had happened. The foreman, ears ringing, just stood there silently opening his mouth like a large fish in a small aquarium. They all heard the sound of metal scraping against wood and turned to see Ma bracing the gun on the front windowsill and taking aim at the middle of the group. In her mind they seemed to be planning another attack on her house. She had to act quickly. Luckily, by the time the blast came, most of the G.P.L. crew had reached their truck which had already started moving away from the scene of the gun play.

Ma's second shot missed the bridge and nearly hit her neighbour's dog, Simon, that was sleeping in an old milk carton by the side of the road. She laughed as she saw two of the men still running down Gordon Street trying to catch the G.P.L. truck. Ma sat by the window trembling with excitement. For the first time in her long life she felt proud of herself. She had not only stood up for herself, but for all the poor people who over the years had been unfairly harassed by the electricity corporation. She was glad that no one had been injured, especially Simon. Ma knew she would get into serious trouble and that the police would soon come and arrest her. However, she was at peace with herself. She had designed a proper ending for the Amelia Mary Bancroft story and she was ready to sleep forever.

The Old Hunter

*T*he moon swam lazily into the vast sea of the sky leaving the trees like sad friends waving on the shores of the horizon. It would be a long night. High in the tree the Old Hunter sighed. It was not a sigh of discomfort or displeasure, but that slower breath that we sometimes take every five or six minutes when we are alone. It was as if he was clearing the mists from his mind so as to recognise his thoughts more easily.

It was Saturday night again and for most of his seventy-odd years the Old Hunter had spent at least one night a-week hunting in the forest. He knew the sweeping freedom of the savannahs and the excitement and drama of drifting down nameless creeks and rivers while hunting at night. But what he treasured most were these nights alone in the forests, listening and waiting.

Most people completely misunderstood this concept of hunting. They complained that it was cruel and unfair to ambush unsuspecting animals in the night as they sought their food. The poor creatures had no chance. The Old Man knew differently. He knew that with so many wild fruit trees bearing in the forest, the chances of animals coming to feed near the place where he sat were quite slim. They could very well decide to have dinner at home for a change. Those non-hunters, although taking careful aim, had badly missed the whole reason for hunting. It was not just about killing animals, but also about spending a few hours each week alone in the solitude of the forest, consulting with your soul, one on one. Events of the past week could be analysed to find the direction and focus of this precious life that we must share with the rest of mankind. The Hunter shifted his position gingerly and listened.

The plaintive cries of the forest night mingled with the sweet smell of damp, decaying vegetation, were like a tonic to his tired, ailing body. Surprisingly he still seemed to hear the sounds of the forest with the same clarity as when he was a boy. Maybe he had just memorised them and now played them back in his mind every Saturday night. These sounds had always amazed him. They seemed anonymous yet distinctive, orchestrated yet random, and after all these years he had still not discovered the sources of most of them. Bird, reptile, animal and insect all had their say and always in the background, that long-winded conversation of the breeze with the trees.

The hunter heard a soft rustling in the thick bushes off to his right and was immediately alert. After a short while the sound faded, but his mind remained focused on the age-old conflict of predator and prey, man against beast. In this forest environment, he reasoned, it was more like beast versus beast, matching their natural instincts and cunning against each other.

The old man often wondered what the animals thought of this whole hunting affair. Did they relish the thrill of the chase as he did? Maybe not. Did they enjoy competing against this strange, dangerous beast who cleverly concealed himself in the forest to attack them? To the hunted, this was no game. The stakes were too high. They faced the ultimate defeat, the forfeiture of life itself, something they could certainly do without. However, there was one thing of which the Old Man was definitely sure. Animals preferred to be hunted in any fashion, rather than face the slow starvation caused by those other, larger, mechanical beasts that removed their habitat, destroying both their shelter and their source of food. If they had a choice, wouldn't it be better to have a sporting chance? If they had to face death, wouldn't it be better near the hollow tree or in the clearing on the bank of the creek where floating fruit sometimes came to rest.

A loud scream pierced his thoughtful wanderings and his heart sprang to life. There was nothing like those primeval sounds to get his old heart drumming with a regular rhythm again. It was one of those anonymous sounds and the only thing remotely resembling it he had ever heard was a mad woman's scream on a city pavement, just before Christmas. The forest sounds settled quickly as the red Bauxite dust had done on the road the day before, after the truck had passed.

It was the coldest time, but the night would soon be over. The Old Hunter detected that subtle change in the sound of the forest insects that usually occurred between four and five o'clock each morning. The reason for this had always intrigued him and he wondered whether

A moonlight night in the forest

it was just a simple shift change between the night and day insects. He shivered and thought that if insects also shivered this might account for the change in the sound of their voices. The hunter had long ago resigned himself to the fact that, in this life at least, there would always be more questions than answers and this would definitely be one of those unanswered questions.

A short distance ahead of where he sat there was a rent in the black lace of the forest canopy. Through this space the Old Man noticed the tell-tale tinge of orange that usually washes the sky before dressing it in morning blue. It was reassuring to know that the gentle fires of the dawn will always melt even the darkest night. The hunt, or as he preferred to think of it, his weekly communion with nature, was almost over.

The morning rushed quickly forward. The Old Hunter got up out of his hammock, stood on a large branch of the tree and stretched his cramped legs. His circulation was not what it used to be, but it would still be some years yet before he would have to stop hunting altogether. He untied his hammock, rolled it up and threw it on the ground under the tree. He had noticed recently that he was experiencing some difficulty in climbing to and from his perches in trees. However, this particular tree posed no problem for him. The Old Hunter took his gun in his left hand and began to make his way down from limb to limb, as he had done for so many years.

The exciting, familiar blast of his shotgun filled his ears, but he felt no impact or even his body hitting the ground. He would never know exactly what happened. Was it the termite-eaten branch that gave way under his weight or did his injured left knee finally betray him? The Old Man lay beneath his tree in perfect harmony with the dry leaves around him. They also had led a satisfying life.

The Old Hunter spent his last moments in thankful prayer. After all, it is not often that a man's life comes to a peaceful, painless end surrounded by the things that he has come to cherish. He noticed the clouds overhead drift behind the trees, but they seemed to move more slowly now, until they paused and settled over his eyes.

GLOSSARY

ACOUSHI ANTS	Leaf-cutting ants that can strip a tree bare overnight.
BACKDAM	On the coastlands it refers to the mud dam separating the farmlands from the water conservancy. In the interior it means any distant work location.
BACKTRACKING	The process of travelling illegally to a foreign country.
BEER GARDEN	Roadside shop where people gather to have a drink.
BOX KITE	A kite in the shape of a rectangular cube.
BUSH BOTTOM	A remote location in the forest.
BUSHMASTER	Guyana's largest poisonous snake. Its bite is usually fatal.
CHILE MUDDA	Term used by a man to describe the unwed mother of his child.
CORIAL	Amerindian canoe made from a hollowed out tree trunk.
CUT EYE	A look of disdain.
CUTLISH	A cutlass or machete.
DAYCLEAN	Dawn.
DREAD-LOCKS	Long braids of Rastafarian hair
FATFOWL	The practice of giving money or buying food and drinks for women in an effort to woo them.
FINE BREEZE	Very small rough diamonds.
FLATTIE	A small, flat bottle of alcohol.
KABOURA	Species of biting black fly that inhabits the savannah region.

KIDDY	Small container used by prospectors to keep diamonds.
LOGIE	A small dilapidated dwelling.
MASHRAMANI	Name of Guyana's Republic Day celebrations.
OBEAH	Local form of spiritualism
PIAIMAN	Amerindian witch doctor.
POINTA BROOM	A broom made from the dried mid-rib of the coconut leaf.
PORKNOCKERS	Early gold and diamond prospectors who got their name from the pickled, salted pork which was their staple diet while in the interior.
RASTA	Short for Rastafarian. A sect noted for the uncut, knotted hair of its followers.
SEE FAR	To predict the future.
SHOUT	A large discovery of diamonds or gold.
SKYLAB	A space station that orbited the earth in the 1970s.
STICKLE	A cyclist balancing in a stationery upright position.
STRANGLER FIG	A parasitic plant that grows on trees in the rainforest, which eventually stifles its host.
SWEET' OMAN	A married man's mistress.
SUCK-TEETH	Sound of disgust made by drawing air between one's tongue and teeth.
TRAMPERS	People dancing in the street at Carnival time.
WARISHI	An Amerindian woven basket for carrying heavy loads on one's back and shoulders.
WHITE MOUTH	A vitamin deficiency sometimes found in undernourished children that causes whitening at the corners of the mouth.

NOTE: The photograph on page 147 was taken by Luana Fernandes, all others were taken by the author Robert J. Fernandes.